MONKEY SEE

A Ben Gallagher Mystery

ALSO BY PAULA LaROCQUE

Chalk Line, a Ben Gallagher Mystery

The Book on Writing: The Ultimate Guide to Writing Well

On Words: Insight Into How Our Words Work—and Don't

Championship Writing: 50 Ways to Improve Your Writing

MONKEY SEE

A BEN GALLAGHER MYSTERY

PAULA LaROCQUE

GREY & GUVNOR PRESS

Dedication

To my great friend Linda Swift—
who, if the truth were known . . .

AUTHOR'S NOTE

Although *Monkey See* is a work of fiction, the murder cases my make-believe killer copies are real and their details faithfully rendered here. Should readers wish to know more about those cases, they could do an Internet search for the Halls-Mills, Axeman of New Orleans, Mary Bell, and John List cases.

Portofino, Ben Gallagher's favorite Arlington restaurant, also was real, once. It was at its Lincoln Square site for 20 years, and these pages are also true to its details—down to the late-summer migratory birds that darkened the sky there by the thousands. Portofino was our favorite restaurant, too, and we've missed it. So it was fun to bring it back to life—even if only for the duration of *Monkey See*.

Paula LaRocque
Arlington, Texas

MONKEY SEE

CHAPTER ONE

Monday morning, August 20

They lay on their backs beneath the August sun. Man and woman, side by side, heads slightly downhill. To Ben, they seemed profoundly uncomfortable and indecent—although every murder scene was at least uncomfortable and indecent.

Ben waited at the crime scene tape, willing the photographer to finish, willing all the first responders to finish—so he could finish, too, and lay these victims level, close their eyes, and cover their faces.

The bodies were posed. And they seemed somehow *dated*. It was subtle—maybe in part their dress. But the setting seemed dated, too—old church, old churchyard. Even the rambling roses nodding on the iron fence suggested another era.

A sudden stiff breeze, Texas hot even in the morning, pressed Ben's damp shirt against him. Realizing he was no longer in shade, he stepped back into the shadows of a gnarled oak. Both sun and temperature had moved higher while he'd waited at the crime scene tape, lost in thought. *Lost in thought.* It was a good expression—and an understandable effect of certain murder scenes. Some scenes readily revealed their secrets, and you weren't lost—in thought or otherwise. Others, like this one, were mute, yielding one overriding question: *What the hell happened here?*

Ben felt that question from his fellow investigators, carrying out their duties in odd quiet.

13

Several big Texas crows swooped low and landed near Ben's feet. They folded their shining wings and swaggered closer to gaze at him, heads cocked in curiosity and eyes black as oil.

"You guys git," Ben said. "Stay away from my dead people."

The crows looked at the bodies and at each other and back at Ben, their yellow beaks gaping. Ben smiled. The birds looked impressed—as if they wanted to say something like: *Well, I never!*

The police photographer ducked under the yellow tape and waved a hand over the scene.

"All yours, chief."

#

Detective Kenechi Akundi finished with the man on the mower and headed up the rise toward the bodies. His suit coat was flung over a shoulder, and deep crescents of damp darkened the armpits of his shirt. His black face shone above the shirt's stark white, and the slash of scar beneath his eye lay like a purple streak of lightning across his cheekbone.

He paused at the top of the rise to inspect the terrain. The victims lay in All Saints' old churchyard amid ancient tombstones. The stones were helter-skelter, their shoulders and inscriptions eroded with age. A stout little crabapple tree stood at the victims' feet and at their heads, a seven-foot stone angel silently blew a ram's horn.

Ben stood with his back to Kenechi. Leaning against the stone angel, his arm draped over its shoulders, he scrutinized the crime scene from behind shaded glasses.

Ben Gallagher, Kenechi thought, hip-to-hip with an angel.

He wasn't quite sure why he was here as Ben's No. 2. All the desk officer said was that Ben needed him on the case. No word of Ben's partner, Jack Malone, a veteran cop of increasing mystery. There were whispers, but all Kenechi knew for sure was that bad blood had developed between Ben and Malone.

Kenechi studied the way his boss leaned against the stone angel, the way he repeatedly shifted the weight of his tall frame from foot to foot. He'd noticed earlier that Ben was favoring his back—something Ben didn't talk about. So Kenechi didn't mention it, either. He studied Ben's strong-boned profile. It was a face just short of ugly that somehow came across as handsome. Deep vertical lines scored Ben's cheeks, cheeks that seemed pale beneath jet-black, stick-straight hair and startling cobalt eyes.

Lincolnesque, Kenechi thought.

Cadaverous, others said.

Ben's coloring was a bequest from his mother—one of many. Nell Gallagher was an heiress. And her wealth was yet another thing a resentful force could hold against Ben since his promotion to chief of detectives. Youth and brains and *money*, too?

Odd that having a brother in Huntsville Prison hadn't proved to be another stick to beat Ben with, Kenechi thought. Instead, any mention of Andrew Gallagher the Convict was matter-of-fact and without malice. *Fact:* Ben's brother was doing ten years' mean Texas justice. *Fact:* booze and grass and college kids and somebody died. *Fact:* Damned shame.

Kenechi had noticed this paradox before. Cops could be sentimental, even mawkish, one minute; hard and mean the next. Maybe the cop/convict angle appealed to their sense of irony. Or maybe it just brought Ben down a bit, tarnished his golden boy image.

Looking at Ben now, Kenechi didn't see a golden boy. He saw a tall, thin, lonely-looking man leaning on a stone angel with a horn.

"Blow, Gabriel," Kenechi said.

Ben turned. "Dr. Akundi. Anything from the yard guy?"

"Nothing new. He's spooked. Almost rode his mower over the bodies."

Ben paced an ever-shrinking perimeter around the bodies, a spiraling search starting thirty feet out. Stepping close, he lifted his dark glasses to study the victims, and Kenechi noticed again how startlingly blue those naked eyes.

Both detectives silently surveyed the crime scene. The bodies lay face up, fully clothed, legs together like storefront mannequins, feet pointing toward the crabapple tree. Stiff with rigor mortis. An old-fashioned, battered gray fedora covered the man's face. The woman, flecked with dried blood, stared directly at the sun with dark eyes as opaque as slate. Small bits of paper were strewn over the couple and the manicured grass . . . or at least manicured to the point where the mower guy saw the bodies.

"Victims three and four," Kenechi said.

"No doubt about it."

"And nothing in common with the others."

"Not a damn thing. Except all are dead."

Ben paused.

"Weird, that hat," he added. "This scene look familiar to you?"

"Familiar?" Kenechi pondered. "No."

Wearing latex gloves, Kenechi picked up a few scraps of paper, read unconnected words that said nothing, dropped the fragments inside a plastic evidence bag, and flipped open his cell phone.

"I'll get these bits collected, see if we can reconstruct them. Wind's picking up. Can we hope for rain?"

Ben shrugged. It seemed there was never a time that Texas wasn't in the middle of yet another drought.

He knelt carefully beside the dead man, knees creaking, back giving off some warning pops. He looked up at Kenechi.

"Long as you have your phone out, go ahead and call 911. Tell them to come get me off my knees."

"You're the oldest young man I ever knew. What will you be like at forty?"

Ben leaned forward a little toward the dead man. It was a small movement, but he gasped.

"What," Kenechi said.

Ben grimaced.

Kenechi bent swiftly, retrieved a wallet from the dead man's inner pocket, and handed it to Ben.

"What's the deal with your back?" he asked.

"Hurt it when I was a kid," Ben said dismissively and pulled a business card from the dead man's wallet. "Shit."

"Vic's name is Daniel," Kenechi guessed. The name on the note.

"The Reverend Doctor Gaylord Longstreet Daniel, to be exact," Ben said. "Episcopalian priest."

"Can't say we weren't warned."

CHAPTER TWO

Ben studied The Reverend Doctor Gaylord Longstreet Daniel. Three-piece navy blue suit, white shirt bloodied but still crisp with starch. Vest and suit coat buttoned. Red silk tie tacked at the middle with a small gold cross.

Ben lifted the fedora from the man's fleshy face. Late forties, early fifties. Touch of gray at the temples. Shot once above the right ear, exit wound at the neck. A burn rim around the bullet hole, the wound star-shaped from the explosion of gases between bone and skin. Not a lot of damage. Something small caliber, the gun touching flesh or close to it when the shooter pulled the trigger.

Ben replaced the fedora and turned to the woman. She wore a short black summer dress and black T-strap heels. Her head rested on the man's outstretched arm, her left hand on his thigh—a hand that looked varnished in the browned red of dried blood.

Compared to Gaylord Daniel, she looked battered. Shot three times at close range that Ben could see—under her right eye, above her temple, behind her ear. And . . . here was a difference: throat slashed, mouth open, deep diagonal cut on her lush lower lip.

Determined flies—ever the *real* first responders— swarmed the wounds, drawn by the smell of blood and human waste. Ben stifled the impulse to wave them away. Insect activity yields important evidence. And flies play their part by laying eggs in wounds and body cavities—eggs that in a given time become maggots and help determine time of death. Ben also knew the heat of a Texas August would speed insect activity and therefore the corpses' decomposition. Part of the equation.

He lifted the woman's earlobe with his pen. Clip-on earrings, securely in place. No struggle.

He studied her jewelry—sterling cuff bracelet and watch, onyx ring on the middle finger of the right hand. Fingers on the left hand unadorned. Wedding and engagement rings? If she'd been wearing them, did the shooter take them?

A black leather handbag rested beneath her right hand. Ben pressed its clasp with a gloved finger and extracted a wallet. A clutch of twenties, credit cards, a driver's license.

Kenechi said, "Craven. Right?"

Ben nodded.

"Claire Craven. Born December 1, 1965. Residence 112 Cain Place. Cain Place. Does that ring a bell?"

Ben ransacked his memory but came up empty-handed. He'd known Arlington streets well during his days on patrol, but like many Texas cities, Arlington was growing so fast it was hard to keep up with the changes.

He lifted his sunglasses again and studied Claire Craven. Her lips still bore traces of dark red lipstick, and they looked garish in the tallow-pale of her face. Contemplating the cut on her lip, Ben leaned forward and peered into her open mouth. Darkly clotted blood inside, like jelly.

He looked up at Kenechi.

"Tongue's cut out."

"She got the worst of it. Think she was the target?"

Ben regarded the woman's dark hair, shining against the grass, her wide dark eyes and high cheekbones. *Claire.* He'd always liked that name, the simplicity of it.

19

He opened his notebook, uncapped his pen, recorded something in his tidy script, and pointed his pen at the fedora.

"That hat."

Kenechi nodded. "Old and beat up. Odd for a snappy dresser."

"The shooter's? But why bring an old-fashioned fedora to the killing field?"

"Beats me." Kenechi paused. "No struggle. Think the vics knew the shooter?"

Something caught Ben's attention, and he carefully lifted a fold of Claire's short black dress. Beneath it, on the grass, lay a handful of velvety circlets of red.

Rose petals.

He opened his notebook to a clean spread. With quick movements, he sketched the bodies, the stone angel, the crabapple tree with its dainty oval leaves, the red roses trembling on the iron fence between church and churchyard. His colleagues would take photographs and measurements, but nothing recalled a crime scene to Ben's mind with more exactitude than his own drawings. When he looked at this sketch later, he'd feel the sun on his back and the damp of his shirt. He'd smell the new-mown grass and hear the cicadas' scream, the investigators' murmur, the traffic on Temple Way, and the planes on their flight path to Dallas-Fort Worth airport, a handful of miles north.

Disorder and early sorrow, he thought, recalling the title of a Thomas Mann story he'd read in college. Here, as in all murder scenes, was Mann's disorder and early sorrow—the chaos of violence.

He looked at Kenechi. "Was the rectory address on the minister's card?"

Kenechi fished the card from its bag and handed it over. Ben read that the Reverend Gaylord Daniel was pastor of All Saints Episcopal Church—*this* church—on Temple Way Boulevard in Arlington, Texas. His residence was the nearby rectory.

"Flushing," Ben said. "That's a short street right around the corner. Let's check it out. Who's available?"

"Coy Ellis and Charlaine Clayton."

Ben smiled. "I never say no to Charlaine Clayton."

Ben knew this neighborhood—it was a couple of miles north of his own place on Aycliffe Court. He often strolled these quiet streets with Mr. Bood, who strutted at the end of his leash, his woolly black coat a profusion of curl and cord, tossing his dreadlocks as if pedigreed and not a mutt found in a crackhouse.

Together, they'd checked out the old churchyard and the crooked gravestones—which dated from 1875 to half a century later. None of this area was urban then, but now Arlington, sandwiched between Dallas and Fort Worth, was part of a megalopolis. And Temple Way Boulevard, minutes from Interstate 30, cut through areas of commerce in both directions.

Avoiding the commercial areas, Ben and Bood would march north on Fielder, turn at All Saints' churchyard and cross back over Temple Way, retracing their steps south beneath a canopy of trees. Ben admired the church's imposing gothic structure, tall spire, and somber stained glass windows. He always felt that the deep tones of stained glass embodied not only myth but also the deeper meanings of metaphor. An unclothed couple banished from a garden. A father preparing to sacrifice a son—prefiguring another

21

such sacrifice. A message from an angel. Three men following a star. An infant born and a god crucified.

Stained glass: Christianity's CliffsNotes.

The arrival of the medical examiner and ambulance crew broke Ben's reverie. They clambered with their body bags and gurneys over the rise, lugging crime scene equipment, steering clear of the old gravestones.

First things first. Ben rose with difficulty and hit some buttons on his mobile.

Was there a *Mister* Craven? Or a *Missus* Daniel?

CHAPTER THREE

There wasn't a Mrs. Daniel, but there *was* a Mr. Craven, and it was almost noon before Ben and Kenechi caught up with him, having made an unnecessary trip to the Craven residence on Cain Place. Now they were back at All Saints, where they found Duff Craven—and a gathering crowd of curious neighbors. Although the neighbors stared at the detectives with open interest and jostled and pointed, they stayed back from the yellow crime scene tape encircling All Saints.

Duff Craven was on the northeast side of the church building, deadheading the roses on the iron fence separating churchyard from graveyard. He had his back to them and didn't turn when Ben said his name. But the snip-snip of his pruning shears slowed.

"Mr. Craven," Ben said. "We looked for you at your home."

"I had to identify my wife's body. And Father Daniel's. He didn't have family." He still didn't turn. "Work to do here, anyway."

Tall, rangy, and gaunt, he wore worn gray denims and a shapeless straw hat. His back and shoulders were rounded as if with the weight of his large head. And he moved slowly, deliberately, as though moving hurt.

Ben could identify with that.

Craven ran his hand lightly over the flowers, avoiding the thorns, seizing each spent bloom between knobby fingers and clipping its neck.

"Just deadheading for now. I hard-prune when blooming season ends. Need more than these secateurs." He gestured with the pruning shears. "But I cut back damaged canes any time. Soon's I know they won't be coming back. Like that one." He pointed his shears at a heavy, barren cane. "I'll need my lopper for that."

The long-handled cutting tool lay on the flagstones behind him, atop a pile of other gardening tools—shovel, rake, splitting ax. Kenechi bent, picked up the ax, and said something to Duff Craven—something Ben missed because of the roar of a jet plane going aloft. Ben shaded his eyes and watched the shining silver Goliath mount the sky against the wind. It passed directly over them, its voice trailing, its nose thrust toward the sky. Ben watched a moment, listening to its long diminishing roar. His own place on Aycliffe Court lay beneath this flight path, so he was accustomed to the planes enroute from and to DFW Airport.

Some people hated living in a flight path. Ben loved it.

"I planted these roses fifteen years ago," Craven said over his shoulder. "About the time Father Daniel came. Planted them at my home, too."

He paused.

"Claire didn't like roses, especially red roses."

Ben thought of the scarlet petals beneath Claire's skirt.

"If she didn't like them, why did you plant them?"

At last Craven turned. He took off his hat, revealing damp hair plastered to his forehead. He was haggard and colorless, face and eyes and hair and shaggy brows as gray as a sidewalk.

"It was the thorns," he said. "But most beauty hides thorns of one kind or another."

"You planted them because of their thorns?" Kenechi asked.

"I planted them in spite of their thorns, but it's not worth talking about. You're the police, aren't you, here to talk about Claire? Or would you rather talk about roses?"

Ben and Kenechi exchanged glances. Duff Craven was controlling the interview.

"Yes, we're here to talk about your wife," Ben said. "And you can start by telling us why she didn't like roses."

Craven turned his pallid eyes on Ben, and in their depths Ben saw not only despair but also challenge and command.

"What about my whereabouts last night?" Craven asked. "When did I last see my wife? How would I characterize our relationship? How did she feel about having a decrepit husband fifteen years her senior? Did she seem normal in recent weeks? Anything happen that might shed light on her death? Did she have any enemies? What was her connection to Father Daniel? Why didn't I call the police when she didn't come home last night?"

"Now why couldn't we have thought of all that?" Ben said. "We'll get to those questions, Mr. Craven. But first, tell us about the red, red rose."

"What, specifically?"

"Specifically, why your wife didn't like them."

He sighed—whether in resignation or exhaustion, Ben wasn't sure.

"The rose has a mixed-up history," Craven said at length. "Confused. Like some people. The early Christians associated its five petals with the five wounds of Christ. The red rose was the symbol of the early Christian martyrs."

Craven turned and again ran his hand over the blossoms, causing a shower of velvety petals.

"Maybe Claire was martyred, too." He pointed his shears toward the tall stained glass windows on the long wall of the church. "Like them."

Ben and Kenechi stepped back a little, the better to see the windows. Each depicted a different sort of violence—a stoning, beheading, crucifixion.

"Did you notice the rose window above the front entrance?" Craven asked.

"That big round stained glass window? That's called a rose window?" Kenechi asked.

Craven pulled at his lower lip. "I don't know which Claire hated more, the red rose as a sign of the virgin or the red rose as a sign of the Holy Mother. But it was also the symbol of Aphrodite and Venus. Goddesses of love. Which didn't thrill the church fathers. And the fathers ruled in those days."

"But the rose prevailed," Ben said.

A flicker of smile touched Craven's colorless lips.

"Roses always prevail. They're not delicate, you know. They allow that myth because it lessens expectations. Like women."

He peered at Ben from beneath his shaggy gray brows. "You know what happened after the explosion at Hiroshima?"

Ben returned his gaze in silence.

"Crabgrass and feverfew sprouted between the broken slabs of concrete, where nothing should have grown. Roses wouldn't be far behind."

Ben pulled out his notebook and wrote something, Craven watching.

"You know the expression *sub rosa*?" Craven asked.

"Under the rose," Kenechi translated. "To keep secret."

"Ancient Romans used to put a rose on the door when confidential matters were discussed." Craven pulled a soiled cloth from his back pocket and wiped the blades of his pruning shears. "Are we finished? I have to wash up."

"We'll finish inside," Ben said.

Craven gathered the heavy tools on the walk, tossed them into the back of a dusty blue pickup parked behind the church, and bent to grasp the corners of a large bag of gardening soil. The plastic slipped through his grasp.

Kenechi moved to help, but Craven motioned him back.

"It's just my hands," he said.

Again he grasped the bag, this time pulling its corners through his arthritic fists and wrapping the strong plastic around his knuckles. With ease, he lifted the heavy bag from the grass, hoisted it onto his shoulder, and laid it gently on the truck's bed.

Stronger than he looks, Ben thought. And resourceful.

CHAPTER FOUR

All Saints' office was up five stone steps to a Gothic arch inset with a heavy planked door. Craven preceded the detectives up the stair, lifted the ornate iron latch, and gave the door a shove. It screeched against its metal jamb like an exotic bird—so loudly that Ben jumped.

At the same moment, he felt something press against his leg and he jumped again, banging into Kenechi and causing him to grab at the handrail. Winding through their legs was a rough-looking tortoiseshell cat. Craven lifted the animal and stroked its brindled orange and black fur.

"Is he yours?" Ben asked.

The cat stretched in Craven's arms, then leapt onto the flagstones and disappeared inside.

"All Saints' cat," Craven said. "Been here since he was a kitten."

He reached behind them and gave the door a mighty tug, treating them again to its ear-piercing shriek—against which they both winced.

They entered a cool, chamber-like room, daylight streaming through one tall archway that led to an adjoining room and another dimmer but identical archway that led to the sanctuary. Ben could see through that opening the nave's dark wood and deep colors, the intense red of the stained glass windows repeated in the thick carpeting that ran down the aisles.

Craven motioned the detectives to a sofa-and-chair arrangement in a corner of the office and Ben sat, his notebook on his knee. He was aware of a rhythmic clicking in the adjoining room—the sound of a computer keyboard.

"Mr. Craven," he said. "You didn't notify the police that your wife was missing."

"She wasn't missing. She came and went as she pleased."

Kenechi rolled his ebony eyes toward Ben.

"Did she wear a wedding ring?"

"Yes. Why?"

"Describe it for us."

"Wasn't she wearing her rings when you found her?"

"I'll ask the questions. Were you aware of her affair with Gaylord Daniel?"

The clicking from the adjoining room slowed, then resumed.

Craven made an explosive sound through his nose. "An affair? Yes, it would have to be an affair, wouldn't it."

"It's our experience that people who meet for night-time trysts in secluded areas aren't there for a coffee klatch."

"We found fragments of love letters at the scene, sir," Kenechi put in. "There are some sizable scraps, and when you come in, we'll want to know if it's your wife's handwriting."

"I'm coming in? Why?"

The clicking in the other room slowed again.

Craven said, "People were jealous of Claire. Maybe you should be talking to them instead of me."

"Can you expand on that?"

"Talk to Regina Tupp and Lily Tansy."

Ben wrote something. "Who are they?"

"Church secretary and music director. Or better yet, talk to Verlie Mae Cheek."

"Who is?"

"The congregation rumor-monger."

"Where were you last night, Mr. Craven?"

The clicking in the other room stopped.

"Right here. Church supper. We were all here."

"All?"

"The family."

"Both you and your wife were active at All Saints?"

"I'm sexton. Claire sings in the choir. *Sang.* My son Ricky helps out wherever . . . still does altar boy tasks. No, *used* to be 'altar boy.' Now it's altar *server.* Next, it'll be altar *girl.* Not that I object, of course. No, indeed."

"What time did you leave the church after the supper?"

Craven's eyes flared, but he said nothing.

"What time—"

"A bit after eight. Regina and Lily were helping Ricky clean up."

"Did you all leave together?"

Hesitation. "Ricky was cleaning up, as I just said. Claire stayed back."

"Stayed back?"

"Don't ask me why. I mean, ask me if you like, but I don't know."

"What time did you get home?"

"Eight-thirty, nine. I didn't look at the time."

"Did you go anywhere after that? Or stay in."

Craven shrugged. *Whatever.*

Still no sound from the other room.

"Can anyone confirm that you were home during that time?"

"As I said, Claire stayed back."

"Your son can verify that?"

His eyes flickered. "Ricky? I don't want my son—"

A voice from the other room, thin and high, cut off his answer.

"His son *can* verify that."

Duff Craven rose stiffly, crossed to the archway to the adjoining room, and stood like a sentry—facing the detectives, who also rose.

"I don't want—"

A young man appeared in the archway, Ben seeing immediately he was Claire Craven's son. The same dark hair and eyes, deeply set above high cheekbones, the same plump red mouth—a little too red, a mouth like a jelly doughnut. And something else. A pull on the upper lip, the thin white line of a cleft palate scar snaking to his nostril. Young Craven dragged his left foot a little, making a muffled, slurry sound on the carpeting, and Ben saw the leg brace, its leather and metal fittings emerging from Ricky's trousers and wrapped around the instep of his brown ankle boot.

"You should get off your feet, Dad." He put a hand under his father's arm and urged him toward a chair, but the older man pulled away. Ricky turned to the detectives with a gesture that everyone should sit, and Ben found himself staring directly into the young man's unfathomable dark eyes.

"The halt and the lame," Ricky said. "But then you noticed."

The detectives sat, followed by the Cravens, and Ben turned to a fresh page in his notebook.

"Ricky, is it?" he said. "What time did you finish cleaning up after the church supper last night?"

"Didn't take long. I had lots of help."

"How long exactly?"

31

"Exactly. I got home not long after Dad. Nine-thirty, maybe. Whatever," he looked at them defiantly, "he was there when I got there."

The detectives looked inquiringly at the elder Craven, who nodded.

"How did you get home?"

Ricky looked blank.

Ben said, "I assume your father drove himself home in the pickup?"

"Regina and Lily dropped me."

Ben made a note and when he looked up from his notebook, saw a remnant of smile on Ricky's red lips.

"Then what?"

Ricky looked blank again.

"Then what did you do?"

"We went to bed. I have to get up early. I deliver *The New York Times*." He glanced at his braced foot. "I drive OK, and it's a job I can do without getting out of the car."

Kenechi turned to Duff Craven. "And you?"

"Went to bed. Like he said."

"Even though your wife wasn't home."

"We covered that," Ricky Craven said.

"Let me make something clear." Duff rose and turned on the detectives a deliberately piercing stare from under his wild brows. "My son is not involved in this mess. I want him left alone."

Ben's eyes met Craven's. Control meister. He remembered Claire in the cemetery, jellied tongueless mouth, glossy hair against the grass, eyes like slate disks open to the sun. Anger rose in his chest.

"Oh?" he said. "Let me make *this* clear, Mr. Craven. We won't be leaving *anyone* alone. Your wife has been murdered." He jammed his notebook and pen into his pocket. "In fact, I'll make that even clearer. Claire Craven was *brutally* murdered."

Craven sagged a little, and his son drew an audible breath.

The detectives turned to leave, and suddenly Craven was behind them, seeing them out with a mighty yank to the heavy planked door, which screeched again. Craven firmly pushed it closed behind them, its shriek this time accompanied by a decisive *chink* as the latch slipped into place—a sound as menacing as a threat.

CHAPTER FIVE

Monday afternoon, August 20

Ben stared at the white board in his office.

The Reverend Gaylord Daniel and Claire Craven were this lunatic's third and fourth victims in two weeks.

Two weeks and four bodies.

And he was nowhere.

Which was what he'd told the chief when he got back from All Saints. And Rolando Saenz had leapt from his big leather chair with such force that it rolled back and banged the wall.

"Nowhere! What do you mean, nowhere?"

"I mean we've got nothing."

"You've got more than *nothing*! You've got the killer's notes!"

Ben had left the room without responding, Saenz whispering, "Ay yi" and sinking back into his leather chair with a *whuff* of escaping air.

The phone on Ben's desk buzzed and two lines blinked simultaneously. He stepped to the window separating his office from the squad room, caught the desk officer's eye through the glass and mouthed, "Who?"

Sly Scroggins punched a button on his own phone and, looking at Ben through the glass, held up three fingers.

Ben waited with his hand on the phone till it buzzed again, then pressed line three.

"Your mother's on line one," Sly said. "Alex on two."

Ben grimaced. He wasn't in the mood to spar with Alex. But Nell wouldn't call the office unless it was important.

34

"Tell Alex I'll call her back. But I'll take Ma's call. Hang on a sec, Sly." Ben looked at the desk officer through the glass. "Anything from Malone?"

Sly shook his head.

Ben pressed line one. "Ma."

"Wanted to let you know Dayt got in OK last night. Nearly one, though."

With two fresh murders on his hands, Ben had forgotten Dayton was flying down.

"How come so late?"

"Cool front. Shifted the wind to the north."

Ben knew what happened with DFW air traffic when the wind shifted to the north. Incoming planes had to go around and queue up to the south in order to land against the wind.

"Dayt doing OK?"

"Looks tired."

"I'll call him. Ma . . ."

"Wait. How's your back?"

"Fine."

Her silence told him she didn't believe him. But what could he say? *Hurts like a hot poker, Ma. My foot is numb a lot, and sometimes when I walk, it slaps the ground.*

"I hope—" she paused.

"What."

"I hope this case won't interfere with our visiting Andrew. Dayton wants all of us together this time."

Ben did know that. He also knew he wouldn't be making that drive to Huntsville Prison. And he was weighted with regret. Nell would be royally pissed, for one thing, and he didn't blame her. He understood his mother, and he tried not to disappoint her any more than life already had. Over the years of Andrew's imprisonment, he'd watched her become fragile and tentative. Now, with Andrew up for parole, he felt she was holding her breath, not daring to hope the cloud that shadowed their lives could lift. Sunny, irrepressible Andrew once again the bright center of their lives! Would she understand he couldn't leave this case even for a day? She would. She would understand perfectly. And she wouldn't care. Nell had *her* priorities, too—Ben, her cop, and Andrew, her convict. Andrew, her baby boy, wasting his youth behind the iron and rust and razor wire of Walker County's lockdown.

"Let's discuss it later, Ma."

"Nothing's more important than your brother, Ben."

"We'll talk about it later, OK?"

"And we'll have dinner with Dayt tomorrow night? And Alex? You'll bring Alex?"

She caught his hesitation.

"Please tell me you're not screwing that up."

He said nothing. Nell had been an orphan, so saying nothing was always best in the face of her eternal quest for grandbabies.

Line two began blinking again.

"Sometimes," Nell said irrelevantly, "sometimes that job of yours—sometimes that *chief* of yours—pisses me off."

Ben laughed. That was so Nell. It was that lousy chief's fault, that lousy job's fault. In the end, whatever his sin, Ben would be blameless.

As Andrew had been.

"You'll have to tell him so one of these days, Ma."

Sly Scroggins appeared at Ben's window and held up a sheet of paper. In the center, he'd printed in black marker: "Line 2. Huntsville."

Ben rose abruptly. What the hell?

36

"Ma. Gotta go."

She was still talking when he bailed out, pressed line two, and said a terse *hello*.

"Bro."

"Andrew. Scared me, buddy. What's going on? You OK?"

"Sure, fine. Working in the library, doing some research for—guess who—the warden. Need to talk to some police types."

"And that would be me?"

"That would be you. And I was just wondering how often it is that when convicts get access to a phone, they call the police."

Ben laughed.

"I talked with Dayt this morning, too," Andrew added. "So this is my day. Dayt and his magic power of attorney. He told me you're all coming down."

"Ahh, Andrew—"

"He also told me you got a serial."

"Two more bodies this morning. I was just on the phone with Ma. I didn't tell her I can't get away. But I can't."

"Ma OK?"

"Yes, but will you please get paroled and start making babies? Don't laugh, Andrew. She's driving me nuts. She wants babies—any babies, with any mother . . ."

"Get me outta here, and I promise to help out." Andrew sobered. "What's happening with the case?"

"Not a damn thing. Nada. Zilch. Not a single lead."

Ben always discussed his cases with Andrew, whatever policy or protocol. It cleared his mind better than a year in therapy. The best part, if there were a best part, was that Andrew lived with criminals, so nothing about detective work surprised him.

And that, Ben thought, made two of them.

"Do you have a minute, Andrew?"

"Sure. I'm doing research for the warden, remember?"

Ben sat back to talk.

CHAPTER SIX

"Fact is, Andrew," Ben said, "Without the killer's notes, I'd never have linked Daniel and Craven to the toddler J.J., or to the grad student Toby."

"The killings had nothing in common, right?"

"Different weapons, methodology. No discernible connection or motive."

"Think the killer's helping you out a little?"

"I've wondered."

"The notes are addressed to you personally?"

"Yeah. All postmarked Fridays, received Mondays."

"What did they say again? Exactly."

Ben opened his murder book. The notes were short enough. And baffling. The names of the deceased and some weird statement in black marker and block letters. And each a death warrant because the deed was done by the time they were delivered.

He read the latest note to Andrew:

DANIEL & CRAVEN
DECEASED
OH, HONEY, I AM FIERY TODAY.
BURNING, FLAMING LOVE.

#

The first victim was three-year-old J. J. Ruben. Strangled, mutilated after death, his soft, pale hair cut from his scalp in rough, uneven patches, testicles partially skinned—as though the killer had begun and was then distracted—thighs and abdomen marked with the clean cuts of something thin and sharp. Ordinary kitchen shears lay beside the toddler. So did a razor blade. J.J.'s small body was posed, and there was a perfunctory detachment in the crime scene that Ben couldn't put his finger on.

"Jesus," breathed Andrew.

"Hang on," Ben said.

Apparently the killer hadn't lingered over this body to show he "owned" it, that he had power over it—typical of a sick psyche. Rather, aside from the strangling itself, all the damage done to J.J. was posthumous and hurried—the patches of shorn hair, the partially skinned testicles, the bloodless and half-hearted cuts. Like something a distractible child might do to a doll.

Posthumous.

"Thank God for that," said Andrew—the exact words earlier of Detective Hilda Cloy.

And Joe Proudhorse, her partner, had responded tersely.

"Nothing here to thank God for."

That first note came only two weeks ago—Monday morning, August 6. An eternity ago:

J.J.

DECEASED

ARE YOU LOOKING FOR YOUR BRIAN?

"No one knows what to make of this 'looking for your Brian' bit," Ben told Andrew.

Not that they could have stopped the killing even if they had worked it out. According to the M.E., the toddler had died early Monday, the day Ben received the note. J.J. was reported missing from his bedroom Saturday—one day after the note's postmark. And his body was found Tuesday morning behind a stack of concrete blocks in a warehouse in east Arlington.

Carefully planned, even if random.

The second note came a week ago, August 13—also delivered on Monday, postmarked Friday. Ben took one look at the primary school lettering and called Forensics, his heart pumping. And Forensics did what Forensics does— dusted for prints, checked for DNA captured in the envelope's glued flap, carefully unfolded and read the contents in Ben's presence before transferring it from their gloved hands into his.

He had stared at the note. *Serial*, his mind whispered, even as he hoped he was wrong. *Serial*—a stranger's haphazard selection. Repeated but random. No system that a sane observer could detect. All the usual motives suspended—love, lust, loathing, lucre. No motive but madness, and the madness often indiscernible. A detective's nightmare.

He read the second note to Andrew:

TOBY
DECEASED
IF EVERYONE HAS A JAZZ BAND GOING,
WELL, THEN, SO MUCH THE BETTER FOR YOU.
THE AXEMAN

"Freaky," Andrew said.
"I had a thought, Andrew. Could these be quotations?"
"Read them again?"

41

"Are you looking for your Brian. If everyone has a jazz band going, well, then, so much the better for you. Oh, honey, I am fiery today/burning, flaming love."

"Wait a sec," Andrew said. "I want to get this down."

Nothing had happened August 13, the day of Toby's note. But the next evening, a landlord who rented out the other half of his duplex near the University of Texas at Arlington wondered why no one was answering the phone next door. The tenant's car was in his half of the garage. And he'd said nothing about being gone. The landlord stepped next door, knocked, tried the door, found it unlocked. The stench that greeted him backed him off the porch and sent him scurrying to 911.

Toby Lugo, a 23-year-old graduate student at UTA, lay in his bloody bed, face bashed with the blunt side of an ax and skull cleaved with its blade, the ax left behind. Although the front door had been unlocked, a panel on the chained kitchen door had been weakened—with a chisel or something like a chisel—and pushed in. The investigators found maggots in Lugo's wounds and estimated the time of death to be thirty-six to forty hours earlier, during the wee hours of August 13.

Like the note said.

"I need to go," Andrew said. "Let me mull this over."

"Great. Go for it."

#

When Ben hung up, he grabbed his notebook and extracted several pages covered with his small, vertical script. He arranged the pages on his desktop and stared at them moodily. Then he slid a folder from his murder book, opened it, and studied its contents. He picked up the copies of the killer's notes and scrutinized each one before he tucked it back into the folder and slapped the folder shut.

Serial. Ben didn't think of himself as a man of passion, but the word gave birth to something wrathful inside him. The random taking of lives. No motive, which translated to Ben as no reason. Someone for whom murder wasn't a one-time act of passion or a thug's crime of violence—rather, someone who longed to kill and kill again. Just for the killing. For the fun of it, if you could say such a thing. Until he was stopped.

And whatever Nell's opinion of his job, Ben was a homicide detective and proud of it—*chief* of detectives, by god. And by choice. Talking with Andrew had reinforced that. It was true that nothing was more important than his brother. And nothing was more important than his mother. But it was also true that nothing was more important than this: He was a homicide detective. A damned good one. There was a lead in this murder book, maybe in this very folder. All he had to do was see it. There were *always* leads.

And, by God, he'd find them.

CHAPTER SEVEN

Monday afternoon, August 20

Ben's partner, Jack Malone, was MIA. Ben had called him half a dozen times since breakfast without response. Best-case scenario, sleeping it off somewhere, Ben thought. Which, all considered, wasn't a bad thing—not when another likely option was Malone's public disintegration, chief and colleagues viewing the wreckage.

Ben exhaled noisily. Sooner or later—make that sooner—he had to do something about Malone. Something permanent. He'd put it off too long. Last week, a whore caught in a community cleanup spotted Malone at the station and gave substance to squad room whispers.

"Whaddya know," she'd said. "Cracko Jacko. They ain't fired your sorry ass yet? Hey, want some primo? Some yolabowla?"

Malone's hand had flown inadvertently to his pink-rimmed eyes and runny nose.

Yeah, something had to be done. Ben knew it. Shit, the whole force knew it. But Ben also knew what they'd do in his place: nothing. It's the chief's to do, they'd say, give it to the chief.

And Malone would be swallowed up in what he hated most: protocol.

Which made doing something all the harder. Time was when Malone gave his all to the department, and lost everything in the process—wife, two daughters, cozy brick home in the Arlington hills.

Still. Ben knew one thing: He was through carrying Jack Malone. He wasn't carrying anyone who chose not to walk. Not that he wasn't the carrying type. But he already had a full load.

He tried Malone's mobile one more time, and when it asked him yet again to leave a message, he said: "Jack. We need to talk. You know we do."

He wanted to say more, but he was struck dumb with the sheer impossibility of it all. What could he do or say that wouldn't fuel Malone's paranoid imagination and make matters even worse? Throw an intervention? A tantrum?

Through the glass separating his office from the patrol room cubicles, he saw his team gathering up folders and notes and coffee cups and heading for the conference room. More ready for the meeting than he was.

He jumped up and strode to the break room, where he poured a cup of muddy coffee that was not only boiling hot but also undrinkable in every other way. Kenechi Akundi, his own steaming cup in hand, waited in the corridor for Ben. Behind Kenechi marched detective Hilda Cloy, self-described Okie, and her partner, Joseph Proudhorse—both with a fireplug body and hair black as lignite. But Proudhorse's Comanche skin was smooth and coppery, while Hilda's angular cheek was craggy with old acne scars.

Detectives Pratt and Naldo emerged from their cubicles and brought up the rear. Ben watched them come—large and tranquil Pratt, face like a punched pillow, and wiry, excitable Naldo, vibrating like a tapped drum. An odd couple, but partners for so long they had one name: *Prattenaldo*. Their fellow cops probably didn't even know their given names. But they were worth knowing, Ben thought. Foncell Pratt and Chucho Naldo.

Jack Malone had once described Pratt and Naldo as too unimaginative to be anything but good cops. That statement should have wrung a little concern from the rest of them, Ben thought, considering Malone's own fertile imagination. Malone: Imaginative enough to be dirty, imaginative enough to consider his flaws a virtue.

Sly Scroggins, the desk officer, stacked folders on the long table in the conference room while the detectives were in a commotion of getting settled.

"Need me for anything?" Sly hovered, small brown eyes hopeful behind horned-rim spectacles—wanting to be in on the action, Ben knew. Sly's pelvis had been broken in a car chase accident and now, in his thirties, he was consigned to deskwork. Ben, himself in his thirties, couldn't imagine it. But he had his own old back injury, and just thinking about it sent a wave of pain across his rump and down his legs.

"Zack Ruben called," Sly said, "He's back in town and says he can meet whenever you like. Sounded kind of blasted."

Blasted, Ben thought. Yes, how you might sound if your child were murdered.

"Set it up for tomorrow, Sly. Whatever's good for Ruben. Kenechi will go with me."

Kenechi, within earshot across the conference table, passed a leathery palm over his face. His own toddler was J.J.'s age. Ben studied Kenechi briefly, thinking again that it was impossible to ignore the jagged purple crescent that began beneath his right eye, ran over his cheekbone, and angled toward his wide nostrils. Ben knew only that the scar was from Kenechi's African childhood. Machete? Someday he would ask.

"Can you take the meeting, Ken?"

Kenechi leaned forward a bit, cleared his throat dramatically, and the others fell silent.

"According to church records," he began, "The Rev. Gaylord Daniel was an only child who never married and had no relatives. The other vic, Claire Craven, was a parishioner. She sang in All Saints' choir and had a husband of eighteen years. Duff Craven. And a 22-year-old son Richard, called Ricky. Duff Craven identified the bodies."

"Who notified Craven?" asked Hilda Cloy.

"Coy Ellis and Charlaine Clayton."

At the mention of Charlaine Clayton, Naldo sighed. And so, involuntarily, did Hilda Cloy. Ben shot Hilda a sympathetic glance. Unlike Hilda, Charlaine Clayton was unquestionably heterosexual. Not that she brought her sexuality to the office—she was strictly professional.

Charlaine Clayton and Coy Ellis were among the best teams on the force, blending similarity and contradiction. She was soft; he was hard. She was restrained; he was forceful. She was tall; he was taller. She was young; he was younger. She spoke in the soft drawl and broad vowels of West Texas, he in the clipped and nasal accents of the Northeast. Yin and yang.

"Coy and Charlaine are still at the rectory," Kenechi said, "where Daniel lived. Maybe they'll find something. But Ben and I did a prelim, and it looked like your basic bachelor churchman's quarters."

"Which would be?" Hilda asked, looking at Ben.

"Oh, bare and ostentatious by turns. Dark and fusty. Overstuffed stuff aptly named."

"Duff Craven was interesting," Kenechi added. "He's sexton at All Saints. And gardener. Didn't seem too broken up. Shock can do that, though."

He pulled his coffee cup toward him, took a sip, and peered into the cup with distaste.

"Speaking of shock," he said,

The detectives laughed.

"Maybe Craven was used to his wife not coming home at night," Ben said. "We hear from the M.E.?"

"Best preliminary guess: Dead twelve hours or so."

"TOD?"

"Around ten, give or take. But before midnight." Kenechi lifted his cup again, changed his mind, and shoved it aside.

Sly Scroggins tapped on the door with one knuckle and stuck his owlish face into the room.

"Ben. Malone called. Says he has the flu."

The room fell into a pregnant silence.

CHAPTER EIGHT

Scroggins was waiting when Ben left the meeting.

"Chief wants you in his office. Mayor Madden's with him."

Ben rolled his eyes, and Sly grinned.

Twayne Madden. Prototypical good ol' boy. Back-slapper, big spender—Granddad's oil money. Bespoke suits from Savile Row, cowboy hat and boots. Baring his long nicotined teeth, slimy stump of cigar between.

Chief Saenz's door was open, and Ben could hear Mayor Madden's voice as soon as he entered the corridor. The mayor was deaf in one ear and seemed to think everyone else was, too. He bellowed in a phlegm-washed voice that made Ben want to clear his own throat.

That would have been all right. What made Ben want to staple Madden's lips closed was that whatever anyone said, did, or had, Twayne Madden said it sooner, did it better, and had it first.

That would have been all right, too. What Ben couldn't brook was that the mayor was mean. People liked to say that if he were smarter, he'd be dangerous. But Ben knew he was plenty dangerous, dumb as he was.

The chief and Madden were sitting at the little round table at the far end of Saenz's office, a silver pitcher and glasses on a tray between them. The mayor was bare-headed, his Stetson on his knee, his lank taupe-colored hair wound over the top of his head in a comb-over that made him look like a kewpie doll. He was talking full-volume about the tough homicide cases back in Mis'sippi and how *his* police had solved them—with *his* help.

"Are you going to solve this one, too?" Ben asked from the doorway.

The chief beckoned Ben with a warning glance.

"We're just—" bawled Madden. "Gallagher, if you ain't one tall sonsabitch. I swear, if you fell down you'd be halfway home."

Ben sat, trying to ignore the mayor's phlegmy chuckle, trying not to clear his own throat, and failing.

"These murders, Ben—community's gettin' all upset."

"Think how I feel."

"Rolando here says things are slippery as snot on a glass doorknob."

Ben looked at the chief, who lifted his shoulders in a gesture that said: *Not really.*

"We need to stop talkin' to the press," Madden bellowed. "Ever time I look at my paper, I see 'according to Detective Sergeant Ben Gallagher' front and center. Ben Gallagher's startin' to look windier than a bag full of assholes."

Ben noticed Madden's omission of his title "chief of detectives" and his emphasis on "detective sergeant"— something Madden did whenever he could. He hadn't approved Ben's promotion, and he made it clear that he thought someone had done an end run to snare the post for Ben. Maybe someone trying to cozy up to the Gallagher family fortune. Or maybe someone smarter than he, Madden—a major but common offense.

Ben opened his mouth, changed his mind, and opened his notebook instead. It wasn't worth it. Anyway, he'd promised the chief.

He cleared his mind. Doodled a three-dimensional box. Sketched a barred window, a hangman's noose. Drew a little gourd-shaped head with a wide-open mouth, put the screamer's palms over his ears à la Edvard Munch.

"Blah," blared the mayor. "Blah blah."

Ben drew a horse's ass . . . . Turned the page and drew a proper horse, put a saddle on him, a pair of reins. Mentally rode him from the room.

"Ben?" the chief said. "What do you think?"

Ben looked around. Twayne Madden was up, pouring himself some iced tea from the chief's silver pitcher, its sides misted with cold.

"Think?"

"Stop that fucking doodling," the chief said hotly under his breath. "Or drawing. Whatever you're doing."

Ben turned back to the sketch of the horse's ass and tilted his notebook so Saenz could see. Saenz rolled his eyes.

Twayne Madden stepped back from the table, stood there while he pulled on his Stetson and adjusted it with both hands, smoothing his hair at the sides with the flat of his hand, drawing the brim down in front.

"You draw?" he said to Ben around the wet stump of his cigar.

"Ben has a Ph.D in art," the chief said.

"Art history," Ben said.

That almost stopped Madden. But not quite.

"I used to draw. Was good at it, too. Thought I'd—"

"Kenechi Akundi also has a Ph.D," Ben said.

That *did* stop him. Ben could see his mind working. *Kenechi Akundi has a Ph.D? That . . . African?*

The chief impaled Ben on a sharp glance.

"Ph.D," Madden said with a lifted nostril that discounted forever the lofty academic degree. "As I was saying, I used to draw. Thought I'd be an artist before I found my true calling."

"Which was?" Ben asked.

"Politics, o' course. Let's see whatcha got."

Ben tried to turn the page on his sketch, but Madden grabbed the notebook and scrutinized the horse's ass. He tossed the notebook in Ben's general direction, shot him a look as frosty as the silver pitcher, and stomped from the room. Or tried to stomp, the heels of his cowboy boots sinking silently into Chief Saenz's carpet.

The chief gazed at the empty doorway, then at Ben.

"Thought you were going to try harder with him."

#

Ben got home late, ate standing at the kitchen counter, and skipped his nightly walk with Bood, who showed his displeasure by banging into and out of his doggy door. Eventually he gave up and lay at Ben's feet, staring darkly at him from behind his dreadlocks.

Ben bent and tousled his coiffure.

"You in there, buddy?"

Bood tilted his head and listened for the word *walk*.

Ben reviewed his case files and finally turned in, only to toss. At length he clicked on the lamp and flipped through the newspaper, looking for the crossword puzzle. And got stuck on the first word! He was aware that some people worked crosswords haphazardly—filling in what they knew and going from there. Not Ben. He was a systems man. He liked to start with number one and proceed to number two.

Same way he worked his cases. Maybe it was a short-coming, but it was the way he thought.

He stared at number one across. It was a stinker, nine-letters. The clue: "To combine with NH3." So not only must he know what NH3 was but also what it was to combine it with something. He looked at number one down. Should have been easier—five letters. But the clue was "elsewhere [Latin.]" Latin! Why not French or Spanish? Not that he knew how *elsewhere* translated in French or Spanish either, but still. Sure, he could look it up—but that was no fun. He wanted to figure it out, not research it.

He studied the clues for the quadrant's remaining four words across. A five-letter word for the offspring of a lion and a tiger. A seven-letter word for *accuse*. A six-letter word prefacing *wire* or *words*. An eight-letter word meaning cash-strapped. His brain felt like mush. After an hour, the crossword's upper left quadrant was still as blank as the rest of the puzzle.

He tossed the newspaper onto the nightstand and tried to budge the slumbering Bood, who lay atop the blanket and responded with a growl. Ben made room for himself on a sliver of mattress and pulled the sheet around his ears.

Monday. Taken all in all, a hellish day.

CHAPTER NINE

Tuesday morning, August 21

Ben overslept the next morning, skipped breakfast, and arrived at the office cranky, edgy, and empty.

So he was glad to find himself with a little free time at midmorning. The others were on assignment, and he and Kenechi weren't scheduled to talk to Zack Ruben till two o'clock. He decided to grab a bite and use the spare time to check out the victims' addresses.

He was behind the steering wheel before he noticed the folded paper beneath his windshield wiper. He got out, pulled the paper from beneath the blade, and unfolded it. In the center of the sheet were two typed lines:

> *Clueless, aren't you.*
> *Poor little rich boy.*

He looked around, saw nothing, pocketed the note, and climbed back into the car.

First stop: grad student Toby Lugo's place off Sanford. Aside from Ben's brief stop at Duff Craven's Monday, Toby's half-duplex was the only victim's home Ben was familiar with—the other vics having been killed away from their homes. Ben pulled to the curb and studied the neighborhood. There wasn't much to see. The area was old, a patchwork of short streets, a litter of cars along both curbs and in the drives, most of the houses without garages. Still, he got a better sense of the place in daylight than he'd had when it was a taped-up, after-dark crime scene, with neighbors and reporters jostling on the sidewalk.

He drove north toward the streets with presidents' names. J.J.'s parents, Zack and Lulu Ruben, lived on Lincoln and judging from the house and the new BMW in the drive, business was fine at Zack's Fitness Center. Ben pulled into the drive and, on an impulse, went to the door and rang the bell, aware that he was acting alone and against policy.

At length, Lulu's sister, a blonde who looked like she was still in her teens, opened the door. Ben recalled she had a name like Lulu's. Fifi? Mimi? Deedee?

He reached for his badge.

"I remember you," she said. "I'm Gigi Boone."

Ben stepped into a tall entry full of light and flourishing green plants. One wall held a full-length studio shot of an older version of Gigi—Lulu as a bride, turned three-quarters to show her veil and gown, its train puddled at her feet.

"If your sister's not here," Ben said, "I won't bother you, Miss Boone."

"She's here. She never goes out. Not any more." She turned to him, twisting her fingers. "She's asleep. I'm sorry—"

Ben stepped back toward the door.

"The doctor's coming pretty soon," she said.

Ben handed her his card, and she looked at it uncertainly.

"We already have several of these," she said.

Ben smiled. "Well, there's another."

He got back behind the wheel and headed south. The Cravens' neighborhood, like Toby Lugo's, was an older community—populated with huge old oaks and fusty little bungalows. Generous front yards, though, the houses set well back from the street.

He pulled up the slight incline of the drive at 112 Cain Place and considered the neighborhood. Quiet. Tuesday morning in late August, kids back in school.

Ben got out and walked up the drive. It led to a windowless, unattached, two-car garage, painted the same faded beige as the shingled bungalow. The garage door was a third of the way up—probably to avoid trapping the Texas heat inside—and Ben could see the bottom of Duff Craven's blue pickup. The house had that desolate look and feel Ben had seen in many victims' homes. A low roof and wide, empty porch fronted the place. It seemed barren and without function, this large porch where no one sat, where no one waved to neighbors from a swaying swing or creaking rocker or wide wicker chair.

The grounds were another story. They evidenced great care. Duff Craven's red roses banked fence and trellis along the whole length of one side of the drive, thick and high enough to hide the neighboring property. Masses of late-blooming flame-red azaleas covered the bungalow's foundation and crape myrtles separated the lawn from the street. From where he stood, Ben could see that the back fence, too, was covered with red roses.

For Claire Craven, who didn't like roses.

Ben walked back to the car, opened the door, but stood a moment thinking. At length he headed to Cooper Street. He didn't notice the dusty blue pickup that pulled onto Cooper several cars behind him, staying with him when he turned onto Pioneer Parkway.

His stomach had been producing surly but feeble growls, as if giving up hope, and he glanced at the dashboard clock. There was a greasy spoon around here that did a booming business till midday—yeah, there it was. Eula's Home Cooking.

On impulse, he wheeled into the crowded parking lot, the noon sun making ovens of the closed vehicles and striking every shining surface with a dazzle that hurt Ben's eyes even behind his sunglasses. He'd never been here. He didn't trust all-you-can-eat joints—a place where both owner and diner often mistake quantity for quality. He recalled a joke:

Two guys leave a bad restaurant, and one says, 'That was the worst food I've ever tasted.'

'Yeah,' says the other. 'And such small portions.'

Ben jockeyed the unmarked into a small space between two pickups with enormous tires.

Eula's was bare bones—plastic and wood, and plastic pretending to be wood. You could eat at one of the small square tables or take a stool. A fat guy in a stained apron hustled at the counter, Eula nowhere to be seen—probably in the office counting her money.

Ben elbowed himself a place at the counter and caught the eye of the guy in the apron. He acknowledged Ben with a raised finger, laid two plates holding something deep-fried on his wide inner arm, and tossed onto the plates a pair of hard-sounding dinner rolls.

Most of the tables were occupied by small groups. But over in the corner, alone at a big round table, lounged a lean guy giving Ben a hard look. He gave it back. They continued the stare-down for a few seconds, Ben knowing how silly it was, then the lean guy lifted his shoulders in a what-the-hell gesture and looked away, losing interest in the thing he'd started. He was tanned, blond, pony-tailed, and wore a long chamois shirt with beads and fringe across the chest and on the sleeves.

Bet that fringed leather is comfy in Texas August, Ben thought.

The fat guy in the apron came over, order pad in hand.

"Who's that?" Ben asked.

"Who?"

Ben nodded toward the blond guy in chamois. "Tonto."

"What?" The counter man managed to lace the single word with outrage. "How do I know who he is. Daniel Boone with a dye job. Who the hell are *you*, buddy?"

For a split second, Ben considered badging him, but the counter man said: "You a cop?"

"I have a sign on my back?"

The guy swiped a rag across the Formica in front of Ben and leaned in on an elbow.

"That guy comes in here for lunch is all I know. He and some buddies. Name's Lonnie. Lonnie . . . something weird. Can't remember. Eula might. Why, he done somethin'?"

Ben shrugged. "Giving me the fish eye. I wondered why."

The guy smirked. "Lonnie doesn't need a reason for that. Probably knew you were a cop. Like I did. You want something to eat?"

Ben looked at the plates next to him. To his right, spaghetti the diameter of earthworms beneath a veneer of tomato sauce and a gray sphere masquerading as a meatball. Left, a mountain of limp french fries and heavily battered chicken. If he were home, he'd make a bacon and mushroom omelet. Toasted bagel, melted butter running over the sides. His mouth watered.

What he got was chicken-fried steak, a flattened, breaded slab of fried beef covered in gravy as white and thick as wallpaper paste, a mound of fried okra, and a pile of corn in a shallow lake of . . . corn juice, or something.

"Don't put those in the microwave," Ben told the fat guy, who stuck the dinner rolls in the machine and zapped them a good one. Turned to Ben.

"What?"

"Never mind."

He brought Ben's plate over. "Lacefield. Just came to me. Lonnie Lacefield. I've heard him called Lace, too."

"You said he comes in here with buddies. Who, exactly?"

The counter man sucked his teeth. "Guy named Ruben."

"Ruben?" Ben fished out his notebook. "Zack Ruben?"

"The fitness guy down the road? Nah. I know Zack. This is his uncle, I think—kind of a toad-looking guy." He watched Ben write in his notebook and added, "Yeah, and another guy he hangs with is LeRoy Shatto. Bookie. Some other guys once in a while, but those three, yeah. They're tight."

Beckoned by another diner, the counter man hustled away, and Ben pocketed his notebook. The other diners were eating with relish, the food smelled good, and Ben was hungry. He pushed the white paste off the beef and used his knife to tussle away a bite, chewed for a while without any appreciable change to the hunk of meat, swallowed hard, and bit into a dinner roll the texture and resilience of a scrapped tire.

He put down his fork and cast another look around the room—at the diners, chewing away. Including Tonto. Then he stood, took a bill from his wallet, tucked it beside his full plate. And left.

He had to do two things, both concerning food.

He crossed the blazing heat of the parking lot, opened the car door and the passenger window, and standing at the open door, phoned Nell. Her machine answered.

"Ma. We still on for dinner tonight? Portofino? Seven?"

Portofino was Ben's favorite restaurant, a quiet place in Lincoln Square. Ben ate there often—not only was it one of Arlington's best, but it was also just a five-minute drive from his home. And it was going to take something like Portofino to erase Eula's from his memory.

Tonto came out of the restaurant with a toothpick in his mouth and headed for a big black SUV with plenty of chrome. Walked past Ben without looking at him. He was the kind of guy with a thin body and long, slender arms and legs, but a round little gut—like a basketball under his chamois shirt. His moccasins were silent on the lot's gravel surface.

Ben climbed into the blast-furnace of the car and turned the AC on high. He'd collect Kenechi. They'd get to Zack's Fitness with time to spare, which was the way he liked it. But first . . . . He slid into the driver's seat, trying not to touch anything metal, drove to Braum's drive-through and ordered a cheeseburger, fries, and chocolate malt. Drove the warm bag and big cold container to the back of the parking area, and ate.

The dusty blue pickup had backed into a corner space and was almost out of sight between two vans. After a while, it pulled out, turned in the opposite direction from where Ben sat chewing his burger, and slowly moved down the street.

CHAPTER TEN

Tuesday afternoon, August 21

A receptionist at Zack's Fitness pointed Ben and Kenechi toward an outdoor area where Zack Ruben, a muscled blond in Spandex and flip-flops, was cleaning a turquoise pool shaped like the state of Texas. The detectives walked past two inert women in thong bikinis who opened their eyes just long enough to register and discount a white man and black man in street shoes and sunglasses.

"Zack Ruben?" Ben showed his badge.

Zack turned away and pulled the skimmer over the pool's surface, snagging some leaves and a cicada shell, and slapped the net against a small pile of debris. Humidity rose from the pool and dissipated in the dry August heat.

"We're working J.J.'s case," Ben said, gentling his voice.

"Then you saw what they did to him."

"Who are *they*, Zack?"

"Whoever. Whatever."

"Talk to us," Ben urged. "Any traffic here in stuff you can't get over the counter?"

Zack's green eyes, lit by the sun, met Ben's for an instant, then drifted away.

"We're not interested in making more trouble for you, Zack. Right now, we're interested in one thing—finding J.J.'s killer. What do you know about Toby Lugo?"

"Who? The plastic surgeon? Know *of* him, that's all. He did most of the boob jobs you see in here."

"*Toby* Lugo. Hayward Lugo's son."

Hesitation. "Never heard of him."

61

"Ever heard of an Episcopal priest name Gaylord Daniel? A woman named Claire Craven?"

"No."

Ben studied him. "Do you or Lulu have any enemies?"

"Lulu!" He looked uncomprehending. "No. Why? Lulu!" He dropped the skimmer and dragged both hands over his face.

Ben's mobile rang, and he flipped it open. Her voice was high and sweet as a child's.

"Detective Gallagher?"

Ben held up one finger and backed away from Kenechi and Zack, out of earshot.

"Lulu."

"You talk to Zack?" she asked. "My sister. . . I wasn't asleep, just . . . "

Ben lost part of that in a rustling sound and Lulu's long, ragged sigh. He turned his back to Zack, kept his voice low.

"I'm with Zack now."

"Ask him—"

Her words were muffled. He turned and looked at Zack, who was leaning on the pool skimmer again, looking back at him.

"Say again?" Ben said.

"Jiggy. Jiggy Ruben. Zack's uncle."

"I'm going to ask you something. Just say yes or no."

He could hear her breathing.

"Was—is Zack dealing?"

A soft intake of breath.

"Or say nothing if it's yes. Steroids? Growth hormones? Hard stuff? What."

Silence.

"Talk to me, Lulu. This is for J.J."

He waited while she cried.

"Doctor gave me a shot." Her voice muffled now, the words slurred.

"How soon can we talk?"

"I can't stop crying."

"I know. When—"

"He was only a baby. It's like . . . "

The silence was so long that Ben pressed the phone to his ear, but heard only a sound like the distant roar of the ocean. He looked at Zack again, not wanting to say her name.

"Are you there?" he asked.

"It's like a deep deep well . . . ." The words drowsy and indistinct.

"I know." He said again, putting his lips close to the phone and lowering his voice even more. "Lulu," he said. "Call me at this number when you wake up."

"A deep well of tears." The words were barely a whisper.

"Will you do that?"

"Overflowing," she said.

"Can you do that?" he repeated. But there was nothing.

He slapped the phone closed and returned to Kenechi and Zack Ruben, who had dropped the pool skimmer and stood with his arms crossed over his chest.

Ben stared at his wrist. "Interesting watch."

Zack looked at him, surprised. So did Kenechi.

"Where'd you get it?"

"What?"

"The watch. Where'd—"

"I heard what you said." Green eyes narrowing. "What's this about?"

"I'll ask you once more—"

"Graduation present."

Ben gestured impatiently, and Zack slipped the sterling bar from its loop and handed it over. Ben examined the watch, then took a plastic bag from his pocket.

"Record this, Kenechi. Who gave you this watch, Zack? When?"

"When I graduated. My uncle."

"Jiggy Ruben?"

Ben had his full attention now.

"When did he give you this watch?"

"Ten years ago. But he said he'd had it a long time. Said it was custom-made, an heirloom." His face tightened. "For when I had a son."

"What's Jiggy's full name?" Ben's notebook was open, his silver pen poised.

"Why?"

Ben gave him a blue stare.

Zack met the stare, then shrugged.

"Jeremiah Ruben."

"Where do we find him?" Ben wrote Zack's answers and closed his notebook. "We'll have to hang on to the watch for now, but—"

"You guys are pretty goddamned heavy-handed, aren't you."

"You'll get it back."

"That's not the point."

CHAPTER ELEVEN

"What in hell was that about?" Kenechi asked when they were out the door.

"That watch was stolen."

Ben read Kenechi's incredulous silence. *The clock's running on a serial killing and you're fussing over a stolen watch?*

"Let's get on the road first, Ken."

They settled themselves in the unmarked, Ben pulling to the exit and into the westbound traffic. He glanced at Kenechi.

"Whoever stole that watch is a killer, Ken. He killed two men. And got away with it."

The Blum brothers. Men Ben knew and loved. For six years, from Ben's earliest memories to his tenth year, Abel Blum had sat beside him on the piano bench, his gnarled hands showing Ben how to coax music from the keys. Afterwards, Ben would drink hot chocolate with Abel and his brother Amos, who made custom jewelry for a little shop downstairs. The two old men had nothing to show of their childhood in a faraway country—no family photographs or furniture or books or even a cup and saucer—but they told him of their youth with such clarity that Ben felt he'd lived it, too.

"So we talk to this Jiggy Ruben," Ben said. "Find out where and when he got the watch. No, I know what you're going to say. But this *is* our case, and it's a lead. We need to find out if there's bad blood between Jiggy Ruben and J.J.'s parents. I want to know if he has connections to Lugo. Or to Gaylord Daniel or Claire Craven."

"Outside chance."

"Agreed. But better than no chance at all. Look at that watch. See that little scrolled emblem on the face—like an A?" He slipped off his own watch. "Look at mine."

Kenechi held the two watches close to the window.

"That's Amos' mark," Ben said. "He gave me the watch when I was ten. He said he guessed he wouldn't be here when I was old enough to wear it." He paused. "That's when I hurt my back. And it's probably also the reason I'm a cop."

The scene that flashed in Ben's brain had the grainy quality of an old and much-played film: Rushing up the stair to the Blums' place, his finger on the bell, once, twice, three times . . . waiting expectantly at the door, hearing nothing behind it. Opening the tall window at the end of the corridor and climbing onto the fire escape, leaning to peer through the Blums' window, the vista from there the kitchen, a narrow passage, the piano room . . . all of it a tumble of overturned furniture and opened drawers and strewn sheet music. And dark smears. Spatters wherever Ben looked, a full handprint on the face of an open cupboard door and a downward smear as though pointing to the frail figure of Abel Blum on the kitchen floor. In his usual dark vest and trousers, his Trotsky-like spectacles smashed beside his bloodied head.

Ben didn't remember running. He didn't remember falling. But he remembered lying on the staircase landing, looking up at the stained ceiling, unable to move.

Now, Kenechi turned both watches this way and that in the sun streaming through the windshield, admiring them, watching the links meld with snake-like grace.

"Old men then, at least to me," Ben said. "Police figured three perps robbed the shop and apartment, beat them to death. The Blum brothers survived Auschwitz, but they couldn't survive Dallas."

"Killers never caught?"

"Nope." Ben turned north on Bowen and pushed up the visor. "I know what they say about justice delayed, Ken, but justice delayed is better than no justice at all."

"The watch doesn't mean Jiggy Ruben was involved."

"If there's no connection, we won't deal with it. I'll give it to . . ." He made a decision. "I'll give it to Malone."

CHAPTER TWELVE

Tuesday evening, August 21

Ben got to Portofino half an hour early and found Dayton already there, in the small bar opposite the head waiter's station, an open bottle of red in front of him.

"I figured you'd get here early," Dayton said, pouring for Ben. "How's the case?"

"Dancing as fast as I can." Ben saluted Dayton with his glass and took a sip. "Got a lead today. To something, if not this case. Where's Ma?"

"Your ma's meeting us here. I want to talk to you."

Ben looked at him curiously. Same old Dayt, the only father he and Andrew had known—even if often at a distance. Gravel-voiced, steady gray eyes behind rimless lenses, natty in dark suit and crisp white shirt. Ben didn't know a world without Dayton. He had always been there and the dynamic always clear: Nell was the love of his life. And somewhere in the misty past loomed the heroic figure of Ben's father, Benjamin Ryan—the love of Nell's life. The boy who went to war.

"What's up?" Ben added, and knew from Dayton's dramatic pause that it was big news.

"I'm selling my share of the law firm and moving to Dallas. I want to be here. Especially if Andrew's paroled. And Nell and I will marry."

"About time."

The barman came over with a smile of welcome and a bowl of peanuts, lit the centerpiece candles, topped off their glasses . . . . Ben regretted the interruption because Dayton and Nell seldom talked about the past, or about anything personal, really.

"There were always reasons for her to say no," Dayton said when the waiter moved away.

"That Catholic thing."

"Whatever. In her mind at least, she was married to Benjamin Ryan."

"Doesn't make sense." Ben tossed a handful of peanuts into his mouth and spoke around them. "How do you commit to someone who isn't even around?"

"You don't think that's possible?"

"I mean someone who's *dead*."

Dayton showed a hint of smile.

Ben studied the older man, the candlelight flickering on his immaculate lenses and glinting on his silver hair. Not so long ago, that hair was dark. Then salt and pepper. When did it go white?

"I guess I've never been in love," Ben said. "How old were you and Ma when you met?"

"When she became old enough to run her own affairs. Eighteen. Talmadge Palmer was retiring, and she needed an executor. She chose me because I was the youngest lawyer in the firm. I was in my late twenties."

He lifted the empty bottle for the barman to see. "Vietnam was the great tragedy of your mother's life, Ben— besides Andrew going to Huntsville. Then—"

"Then?"

"Then nothing. You know the rest."

This was it. This was where they always closed down.

Ben pictured the vestibule on the second-floor landing of Nell's townhouse. The grandfather clock that had marked time for the Gallagher family for as long as he could remember. The photo gallery documenting the Gallagher boys' infancy, boyhood, college years. A decade of Ben alone—Nell didn't want to look at pictures of Andrew in a prison jump suit. And displayed behind Plexiglas—like the Plexiglas that now separated them from Andrew—was the American flag that had draped Benjamin Ryan's coffin. Alongside the flag was a photo of a late '60s student rally, banners fluttering on the breeze. Two tall, jeans-clad students were in the foreground, dark hair blowing across their faces—Nell Gallagher and Benjamin Ryan, leaning into each other, extending a peace sign.

"Why is Ma so secretive about Andrew's father, Dayt?" Ben asked. "Not that she says much about mine, either, but—"

Dayton's face closed.

"Whatever she wants left alone, Ben," he said, weighing his words, "my counsel to you is to leave it alone. Just take it on faith that she has her reasons."

As little as this was, it was still more than either Nell or Dayton had said. But he felt chastened, and he lightened his tone.

"So. Are you asking me for her hand?"

A tall woman wearing a summer tan, a short white dress, and a wide white smile approached the table.

"Hey," Ben said, managing to pack a lot into one word.

"Hi, Ben." Her soft West Texas accent made it *Hah, Bin*. "No, don't get up. I'm just saying hello."

"Charlaine Clayton, meet Dayton Slaughter." He turned to Dayton. "This lady here's the PO-lice."

Nell—also sporting a white dress and wide white smile—chose that moment to arrive.

"You're on the force with Ben?" Nell asked. Her glance at Ben was half-accusative. A potential baby mama!

Ben looked at the two of them, Charlaine half a head taller than Nell, but with the same ivory skin and bright blue eyes and auburn hair. Ben wasn't used to seeing Charlaine out of uniform—but even in uniform, wearing no makeup except a smear of lip gloss, she was beautiful. The uniform didn't hide the full breasts and tiny waist and shapely ass. It didn't hide her flawless ivory flesh or the faint floral scent of her. And the single long braid didn't hide the curly copper tendrils that framed the pale oval of her face.

The first time Ben had seen the Coy Ellis/Charlaine Clayton team out of uniform was at a Christmas party. Both wore unrelieved black and looked straight from a fashion shoot—Coy slender and easy in a perfectly fitted suit and silk shirt open at the neck, Charlaine in full makeup, loose hair a soft cloud halfway down her back, her short dress and stiletto heels adding to her long legs and imposing height. A glimmer of diamond shone at earlobe and wrist, replacing the Swiss Army watch she wore in uniform.

It was then, too, that Ben first knew Charlaine was from money. Takes one to know one, she'd said later. Maybe it did. She came from Midland-Odessa oil country. And if she also came from oil *money*, she was as discreet about her family fortune as Ben was about his. One thing he knew: The slender diamond bracelet encircling Charlaine's wrist that night cost infinitely more than the Swiss Army watch she wore daily.

Ben found when they danced that in her six-inch heels, Charlaine's head was to his shoulder. Her auburn hair brushed his cheek, her firm body fit well into his, and seemed soft and yielding. But when he tried to gather her closer, she resisted without seeming to—after one long, slow turn, there was more distance, not less, between them. She smiled frankly at him with her straight white teeth and glossy mouth, the smile saying: No.

Ben smiled back, thinking: She's good at this, she's had practice.

Charlaine Clayton. Out of reach. At least for fellow cops.

Nell took her seat as Charlaine headed back to her table and narrowed her eyes at Ben.

"You never told me about her."

"Don't start, Ma," he said.

"I just hope—"

"We know what you hope, Ma," Ben said.

"Oh, crapola. But why not? When I see someone who seems special, who meets certain standards—why are you laughing?"

"Whose standards, Ma?" Ben asked.

"Well . . . mine."

"At least have the decency to look sheepish when you say that."

She smiled.

"Anyway," Ben added, "your standards for a daughter-in-law are hardly a hurdle."

"Who says? You don't even know what they are."

"Yes, I do."

"No, you don't."

"Yes, I do. At least one ovary with a few decrepit but still viable eggs."

"Ahh!" She tossed back her head and laughed. "Lose the *decrepit*, Benny, and we can talk."

CHAPTER THIRTEEN

Ben got home from Portofino about eight-thirty, sorted through his mail, and went into his studio, Bood prancing along beside him, toenails clicking on the hardwood floors. Ben removed the cloth covering the canvas on the easel and dampened it so the oils wouldn't dry out. He stared at the painting, first critically, then pleased. His fingers itched to pick up a brush, a palette knife—no telling when he'd get the chance . . . he covered the canvas quickly and strode toward the bedroom, where he changed into shorts and Nikes. Always a mistake to pick up a brush if he didn't plan to spend several hours at the easel.

Tired as he was, he needed to walk, to loosen up. He'd ignored the ache in his lower back all day, but he knew from experience that if he went to sleep sore, he'd wake up worse. And judging from Bood's ecstatic leaps at the sight of Ben's Nikes, he was ready to walk, too.

"Get your leash, Bood," Ben said, and the dog peeled off toward the garage door, where his leash and harness hung.

They struck off toward Fielder, then toward Temple Way Boulevard, Bood lifting his leg to pee every four feet. Ben admired the way the dog husbanded his resources, rationing his output so that no matter how long the walk, he'd still have a squirt or two left when they turned into Aycliffe and home.

A bracing breeze from the north had supplanted the usual hot, humid air from the Gulf, lifting Ben's spirits. An occasional late jogger chugged by. A dog barked here and there, setting up an answering canine clamor from the neighborhood as well as an anxious little grumble from Bood. Neighbors emerged from the golden rectangles of their doorways and deposited bulging plastic bags on their curbs.

Tuesday. Trash night.

Ben crested the hill leading down to Temple Way Boulevard, and All Saints' Gothic spire and stained windows came into view, the church sedately back from the road. He saw a figure on the sidewalk and crossed the boulevard.

"Working late," he said to Ricky Craven, who was unloading a wheelbarrow laden with black plastic bags.

"Trash from the church supper. Taking care of it for my dad." He wrestled a couple of the large bags from the wheelbarrow and set them on the curb. "You walk late, too."

"A constitutional for my dog and therapy for me. I have a tricky back. Helps if I walk before I go to bed."

A helicopter rumbled overhead, low enough for the percussion of its blades to shake the stained glass windows of the church.

"These aircraft can drive you nuts," Ricky said when the noise abated. "Almost did Father Daniel. Especially during a sermon."

Ben realized that a steady drone of throttled-down jet engines had accompanied him and Bood on their walk.

"Front's hanging around," Ricky said. "The planes have to land against the wind, so you can tell when there's a wind shift. When it shifted to the north Sunday night during the church supper, it was one long din of planes directly over us, queuing up for a landing from the south."

Ben recalled that Dayton's plane had been delayed Sunday night.

The noise from the helicopter faded to nothing, and a wide swath of night sky suddenly went darker with the restless, erratic flitting of bats.

Ben looked up.

"Bats," Ricky said. "Much-maligned night-fliers."

"They coming from the church?"

"From the attic."

Ben smiled. "I suppose I wouldn't be the first to mention that you have bats in your belfry. Do the parishioners mind?"

Ricky didn't respond immediately, and Ben felt rather than saw his gaze.

"If they do," he said finally, "we remind them the common brown bat can eat 600 mosquitoes in an hour."

"Is that true?"

"Yes."

Ben watched the bats roil and disperse.

"Swift and silent," he said.

"They're not silent. The human ear just can't hear them." Ricky spritzed the mound of trash bags with something from a spray bottle, and a pungent odor immediately wafted to Ben's nose. "Lots of mammals suffer that."

"Suffer what?"

"Hearing problems."

"Is that ammonia?" Ben asked.

"Keeps off the foragers. Varmints."

Ben stood back a little from the smell.

"Varmints have to eat, too. And we stole their habitat—speaking of suffering mammals."

"Were we?"

"You were. Why not give the varmints your garbage instead of spraying it with poison?"

Ricky said nothing.

Ben said: "I understand your father's a sexton at All Saints. What does a sexton do?"

Ricky's face was a pale, unreadable oval in the moonlight.

Bood tugged at the leash, wanting to nose at the bag. Ben was about to pull him back when Ricky Craven pointed the spray bottle in Bood's direction. Ben stepped forward, bringing the leash behind him and putting himself between Ricky and the dog. With his free hand, he caught Ricky's wrist and squeezed.

"Spray that on my dog, or even in his direction, and they'll be picking you up tomorrow morning along with the trash."

Ricky grunted, the spray bottle slipping from his grasp and falling onto the mound of trash bags. When Ben released him, he rubbed his wrist and, unaccountably, laughed. Then he turned and mounted the grassy incline, his braced leg dragging a little over the small irregularities of the manicured lawn. Ben watched after him a moment, the rising moon lending its silver light to the shadowed churchyard, the roses nodding on their iron fence, the heavy side door screaming against its jamb as it opened and closed.

#

They got back from their walk a little after nine, Ben's legs throbbing and back aching. The first thing he did was go to the bedroom and retrieve the crossword puzzle he'd wrestled with the night before. He took the folded newspaper page to the kitchen and spread the puzzle on the granite counter, studied the clue to one across briefly—"to combine with NH3." Nine letters.

He printed into the spaces, *ammoniate*.

That made the first letter of one down an A—a five-letter word meaning *elsewhere* in Latin. He frowned in thought but came up with nothing. He refolded the puzzle and poured himself some Chilean red. A chief indulgence, but he kept it under control. He'd seen the slow, degrading slide into addiction of too many police colleagues. Men like Malone, who let drugs or a bottle handle the job's stresses. Heavy drinkers who made it a point of pride to "hold their liquor"—until a day when they no longer held it. But it was a couple of hours since Ben had helped Dayton and his mother polish off two bottles, so he poured a fresh glass and took it outside to survey his gardens under the moon, Bood trotting behind, almost invisible, his coloring so relentlessly black that he drank up the light, reflecting nothing. Even in the light, if his eyes were hidden and he wasn't baring his teeth or showing his little pink tongue, you only guessed that a face was somewhere in that tangle of curl.

They sat on a bench in the side yard under a dark sky pricked with stars, Bood's chin on Ben's thigh, and listened to the occasional roar of approval or dismay rising from the Rangers ballpark and drifting their way on the breeze. Time was, Ben reflected, when he and Andrew and Nell regularly drove I-30 between Dallas and Arlington to attend the Ranger games. Now he wasn't even sure who was playing. Orioles? Mariners?

He heard the first of the post-game fireworks. Unusual for fireworks on a weeknight, must be some special celebration. If he walked a little away from the canopy of live oaks sheltering his cul de sac, he'd be able to see the display in the eastern sky.

But he needed to think.

He turned the case in his mind, its aspects tumbling like clothes in a dryer. Then the bangs, booms, sputters, and whistles of the ballpark's pyrotechnical grand finale began—hushing normal late-summer sounds. There was an instant of what seemed a shocked silence when the commotion died away, then the night filled again with the croak of frogs and the hysterical scream of cicadas rising in rhythmic crescendo.

He looked at his watch, drained his glass and stretched, the light breeze pressing his damp shirt against his chest. A cool front this time of year meant little in Northeast Texas, where humid August nights remind you that you're closer to New Orleans than to El Paso.

Ben collected his trash and set it out on the curb, then turned on his computer, called up a search engine, and typed in "sexton."

"A sexton," he read, "is a church officer charged with the maintenance of the church buildings and/or the surrounding graveyard."

Wikipedia, his best friend. He read a little further.

"The word *Sexton* is believed to be derived from the Anglo-Norman *segerstein* which itself originated from the Latin word *sacristanus* which basically means someone who looks after the sacred objects."

Someone who looks after the sacred objects.

#

He rinsed his wine glass at the sink and went into the living room, Bood at his heels. Ben's favorite spot—quiet and orderly and warmly lit, its lamps timed to go on at dusk. He slipped off his Nikes and plopped into the deep cushions of his easy chair, angled to face the fireplace. Put his stocking feet on the ottoman, reached into the drawer of the lamp table, and withdrew the single item in the drawer: a harmonica.

Bood jumped lightly onto the ottoman and lay with his firm little body pressed against Ben's legs. Ben put the harmonica to his lips, closed his eyes and softly blew a few blues licks, bending the notes. He wasn't in the mood for a tune, so he improvised. Riffing up a groove, as Andrew would say—some slides and glissandos, trills and tremulos, straight eights and shuffles.

At first, Andrew had missed his music.

Can't you have an instrument in here? Ben had asked.

Andrew had grinned. You gonna smuggle in my cello?

So Ben bought him a Marine Band harmonica—little, light, less than fifty bucks.

To start with, Andrew had played only in the yard and off by himself. Then, maybe two years ago, a voice from another cell had called softly after lights out: *Why don't you play something on your mouth organ, Gallagher? Something nice and easy.*

And often, sitting here in the evening, Ben wondered: Is Andrew playing right now? He'd look around his living room—off-white sofa and chairs, gleaming floors, a splash of vivid color from the abstract oil above the mantel. And he'd see instead a tiny, barred space, an iron cot with a thin pad of mattress, an open toilet. And he'd slip the harmonica into

its drawer and head for bed, the weight on his shoulders
nearly ten years old.

CHAPTER FOURTEEN

Wednesday morning, August 22

"Fucking lunatic."

Hilda Cloy sat on the opposite side of Ben's desk, murder book on the desk in front of her, and stopped cracking her gum long enough to send Ben a dark look. Joseph Proudhorse sat next to her, turning the murder book's pages with one hand and holding a half-eaten doughnut in the other.

The mail alert on Ben's computer pinged, and he recognizing the sender as a Huntsville employee who sometimes sent him e-mails from Andrew.

"Hang on a second," he said to Hilda and Proudhorse. He opened the message.

Andrew says check out the following URLs, the text read. Below that, the long strings of three website addresses.

Ben clicked on the first link. A section of newspaper page appeared—a New Jersey newspaper dated September 16, 1922. It featured a photograph and a story headlined "Crime of the Century." Ben sat forward and squinted at the photo. It was small and grainy, but he could make out two bodies, a man and a woman, in something that looked like a field. He made the photo larger.

"Hey *hey*," he said softly.

Halls-Mills, the caption read. *An Episcopal priest and a choir girl lay dead beneath a crab apple tree. Who killed them?*

Hilda and Proudhorse came around Ben's desk to peer into his computer screen.

\#

Twenty minutes later, Ben stuck his head out his door and yelled, "Sly! We need a meet!" Then he hustled down the hall carrying a sheaf of printouts, barged into the chief's office, and plunked the pile of paper on his desk.

"Don't bother to knock, Gallagher," Rolando Saenz said. "Especially if that's a smile on your face."

"They're copycat murders. The original cases are all on the Internet, every detail. All kinds of hits. Even whole—"

"Hang on. What?"

"J.J. One of our vics—the toddler. And Toby Lugo, the grad student. Gaylord Daniel and Claire Craven, priest and parishioner. All here." He slapped the pile of printouts. "Not those names, but the cases. They're copycat killings. Every important detail."

Saenz picked up the printouts and leafed through them. "Goddamn. Good work, Gallagher."

Ben hesitated. "Actually, it was my brother's . . . find."

The chief looked at him over his reading glasses.

"Your brother."

"Andrew. He works in the library at—"

"I know where your brother is, Ben," Saenz said, his gelled raven hair perfectly still under the ceiling fan. "How's come we came up dry when we dug through the case files?"

"Two of the cases are really old. The Halls-Mills case—the template for the Daniel/Craven case—was close to a century ago. New Jersey, 1922. The Axeman murders were even older. Those were in New Orleans, 1911 to 1919. The

Bell case—the J.J. template—was in the '60s, but it was in England. J.J.'s murder is a carbon copy of that case, even to the age of the boy. Even to what was done to his body after death."

Ben paused dramatically.

"Ask me who the killer was in the Bell case, the original case."

The chief cocked a dark brow. "Do I want to know?"

"A ten-year-old girl."

Saenz flinched. "Children killing children. Children mutilating other children's bodies. Ay yi. If it comes to that, I'm looking for another job." He thumbed through the printouts. "We gonna get something from this, Ben?"

"We'll sure as hell try."

"Another thing. You're down a man, and Kenechi needs a partner. Need to do something about that, Ben."

"I know. But I want to make the right pick."

Kenechi's partner had abruptly left the force. A good thing, too, Ben thought. Headstrong and impatient, he'd been a poor fit for police work. He took shortcuts and tried to manipulate people and information—more interested in stamping a case closed than in actually solving it.

So he wasn't a good fit for Kenechi Akundi, either—not for methodical, meticulous, moral Kenechi. Kenechi was a thinker with solid insight into human behavior and motivation—a detective capable of the same sort of intuitive flash Ben was known for. Cops like Kenechi's ex-partner didn't have the time or patience—let alone respect—for that kind of deliberation.

"I asked Charlaine Clayton," Ben said. "She would click with Kenechi. With the team, too. Already has."

Saenz raised his brows. "Perfect. She interested?"

"Not for now. Likes the street."

"I'd hate to lose her as a uniform. On the other hand, she'd shake up the team. Especially Naldo. And Hilda."

He grinned and gave Ben a playful slap on the shoulder.

"And maybe even my chief of detectives."

Ben understood. This was Rolando Saenz's way of glossing over the fact that his chief of detectives discussed the department's cases with his convict brother.

CHAPTER FIFTEEN

Midmorning Wednesday, August 22

"J.J. Ruben, our copycat's first case," Ben said.

The detectives sat tense and erect around the long oval of the conference room table, the bright white light of morning streaming into the windows and draining the color from the gray-green carpeting and painted walls, making them look drab and industrial.

"The Mary Bell case." He waited for them to find the right printout. "Took place in 1968 several hundred miles north of London."

"Is this the vic?" Hilda pointed to a photo on the first page of the printout, a pretty little girl with dark curls crowding her large eyes, lips curved in a beatific smile.

Ben paused for effect. "That's the murderer. Mary Bell. She was ten years old. The victim was three-year-old Brian Howe."

"Are you looking for your Brian," Kenechi quoted softly.

"That's what Mary Bell asked the Howe family when she offered to help them look for the missing toddler," Ben said. "You can read all this for yourself. And you'll see how closely the killer followed the template of the original case. Brian Howe was strangled, like J.J. He had the same weird posthumous wounds—clumps of hair cut away, puncture marks on his thighs, scalpel-like wounds on his abdomen, genitals skinned. Scissors near the body. Same as J.J."

Everyone was quiet. Most of the detectives directed their stony attention to their printouts, but Hilda stared at her small, square hands, clasped on the tabletop.

"I'll let you spend some time with this stuff before we discuss each case detail," Ben added. "It's not pretty reading. For now, go to printout two."

They shuffled the printed pages, eager to tuck out of sight the pretty little ten-year-old girl who strangled and mutilated a toddler, then offered to help his distraught family.

"The Axeman. Template for Toby Lugo's murder," Ben said, holding up a cluster of papers stapled at the corners. "Terrorized New Orleans in 1918 and 1919, attacked fifteen or twenty people with an ax. His M.O. was what we saw with Lugo. Chiseled a door panel to weaken it, broke it out, butchered the sleeping people within. Usually left the chisel and ax behind. Nothing stolen in any of the cases. Most of the victims were Italian grocers. Go figure."

"That freaking quotation?" Hilda asked. "If everyone has a jazz band going . . . ."

"*If everyone has a jazz band going, well, then, so much the better for you.* Word for word from a letter the Axeman wrote to the *New Orleans Times-Picayune*," Ben said. "Which the newspaper printed. It was a rambling warning that the Axeman was a demon in league with the Angel of Death. Said he was going to pass over New Orleans on a certain night and could kill thousands, but that he would spare people in houses where jazz was playing."

"Guess the joint was jumping that night," Hilda said.

"Jazz-loving bogeyman," Kenechi said. "They catch him?"

"Nope. And the attacks stopped as abruptly and mysteriously as they began. It's all here. Plus some theories."

He tapped the thick sheaf of papers and took up another stapled packet.

"The original for our third case—the Hall and Mills case, New Jersey, 1922. Known at the time as the crime of the century, but this was a decade before the Lindbergh baby kidnapping and murder. Hall and Mills are better known to us as Gaylord Daniel and Claire Craven. This case is in some ways the most complex because it's a double homicide. It's also the most faithful to even the smallest details of the original murder. Also unsolved—although, like the Axeman case, there are theories."

The morning sun cast its rays through the blinds directly onto the smudged tabletop, and Hilda rose to fiddle with the blinds.

Ben got up from the table and stretched and grunted. "Who wants coffee?"

Nobody did, so he took his own cup down the hall into the break room and to the coffee urn and, against his better judgment, brought down the black plastic handle. The coffee came out of the spigot in an opaque brown stream, smelling burned.

He looked toward Malone's cubicle as he passed through the squad room. Chair empty, desktop a mess. The usual. Ben shook his head and Sly, noticing, offered him a commiserating shrug.

Back in the conference room, Ben picked up where he left off.

"Edward Hall was a priest at an Episcopal church, and Eleanor Mills sang in the choir. And get this—her husband was sexton at the church."

"Wow," said Hilda.

"Stay tuned," Ben said. "Hall and Mills had been involved for some time in an affair that was common knowledge in the parish. They were found shot to death near a crabapple tree on some abandoned farmland, their bodies posed as precisely as Daniel's and Craven's. Stretched out side by side on their backs, her head resting on his arm, left hand on his thigh. Some 32-caliber cartridges strewn around the scene."

He sipped his coffee and made a wry face.

"Hat over the minister's face?" Kenechi asked.

"Yep. Not a fedora, though. The original was a Panama. Killer probably did the best he could getting a vintage fedora."

"Torn-up love letters strewn over the bodies?" asked Proudhorse.

"Yep."

"*Oh, honey,*" Hilda quoted from memory. "*I am fiery today. Burning, flaming love.*"

Ben nodded. "From the original letters. In the Mills woman's hand."

"The wounds?" Pratt asked.

"Same. Father Hall was shot once, over the right ear—as Daniel was. Eleanor Mills, like Claire Craven, was shot in the right temple, under the right eye, and behind the right ear. Her throat was slashed and, again like Claire, her tongue was cut out. Plus, her larynx was removed. News stories of the day made a big deal of the choir singer whose singing days were over."

"Shooter went to a lot of trouble to match the cases," Hilda said.

"Even to leaving the priest's business card at the scene." Ben stacked his printouts and evened them up by tapping their edges against the tabletop. "But why?"

"Being a maniac is the only *why* a maniac needs," said Kenechi.

"Read all this stuff," Ben said. "See what you can come up with. Remember there are no dumb ideas. And we'll start interviewing now. I'm putting a list together."

Naldo turned at the door. "It doesn't have to be cyber-psycho. Or cyber-whiz, for that matter. Anyone can use a search engine. Or look up murder cases on the Internet."

Ben considered.

"OK, but why? So we'll *think* psycho? Think serial?"

Kenechi took up the idea. "Sidetrack. Cover. To make us think the murders are random when they're not."

"If they're not random, there are connections," Joe Proudhorse said. "We need connections."

Ben met Proudhorse's basset hound eyes.

"Bingo," he said.

#

Ben eased into his desk chair, adjusted a lumbar roll at the small of his back, and looked through the glass at the squad room.

"Have you seen Malone?" he asked Kenechi, who had followed him to his office.

"Sly said he was coming in."

"When he gets here, would you fill him in on the Blum brothers thing? And Jiggy Ruben. Tell him to dig out the Blums' files and go over them. Tell him I'll be in the office later this afternoon and we can talk about it."

Kenechi nodded. "Great work on the cyber angle."

"My brother—"

"I know."

No secrets in a squad room.

"Speaking of your brother . . . ."

"Yes?"

"He's up for parole?"

Right. No secrets in a squad room.

"Kenechi," he said. "I have to see what the chief wants. Then I'm going out to the Lugos with Hilda and Proudhorse."

Ken looked at him expectantly.

"It's . . . can we leave this till later?"

"Sure," Kenechi said. "We can leave it forever."

But his big voice was gentle.

CHAPTER SIXTEEN

Wednesday afternoon, August 22

"You guys run this," Ben told Hilda Cloy and Joe Proudhorse as the Lugos' huge brick-and-stone-and-glass home loomed into view. "I'm just tagging along. Making notes."

Proudhorse was driving, Hilda in the passenger seat, Ben in back, fingering an unread note in his pocket. The second in two days. He and the others were heading for office parking when Ben had ducked into his own car to get his suit coat, noticed the folded note beneath the windshield wiper, and surreptitiously retrieved it.

Now, in the backseat of Hilda and Proudhorse's unmarked, he withdrew the note and read it. Four words typed in the center: *Running out of luck, rich boy?*

Proudhorse drove up the steep incline, pulled into the gated courtyard, parked at the top of another incline, and jerked on the emergency. Hayward and Cecilia Lugo lived high in the hills of northwest Arlington, and the three detectives piled out and took a second to admire the view.

"That clinches it," Hilda said, punching the doorbell. "In my next life, I'm a plastic surgeon."

A small brown woman wearing a maid's traditional black dress/white apron answered the bell, but Hayward Lugo showed up behind her.

"I've got it, Eva."

He ushered them through a game room to a mahogany game table set in a glassed-in alcove and loaded with drinks and hors d'oeuvres. He pointed at the woman sitting at the table.

"My wife, Cissy. Cecilia."

"Sit," Cissy said, rising to make room. She wore a peach-colored caftan that showcased unnaturally large breasts and unnaturally small waist.

"Is this a bad time?" Hilda asked, eyeing the table. Silver dish of crackers and party breads. Several blocks of cheese beneath a crystal dome. A tray of smoked salmon. A pitcher of martinis, and Cissy stirring a Bloody Mary with a celery stick.

"Any time's a bad time." Hayward Lugo picked up his martini glass, pinkie finger extended. "We're leaving Saturday morning for Costa Rica."

As if to prove it, the small brown woman named Eva appeared in the doorway, laden with matching pink leather luggage. She sidled past the detectives to reach the long corridor leading to the master suite. Murmuring apologies, she pulled a large pink suitcase behind her with one hand, held a valise in the other, and clamped a zippered case beneath an elbow. Each of the pieces wore a bronze initial C and a sculpture of a long-stemmed rose.

Proudhorse and Hilda sat well back from the laden game table and took out their notebooks. Ben remained standing and, after a cursory glance his way, the Lugos ignored him.

"I wish we were going on safari instead," Cissy said. "But it's not the same. I used to love safari. Didn't I, Hay? We used to have tons of natives along with us. It's different now."

"They don't measure the natives in tons anymore?" Hilda said, ignoring Ben's glance.

"I need more time in the tanning booth before I leave," Cissy continued.

To Ben, it looked as if she'd already stayed too long. Her face looked baked, what he could see of it. It was obscured on both sides by long, lusterless hanks of blonde hair that curved at her jaws like Saracen blades and was snipped at the forehead into an uneven fringe that veiled her plucked and redrawn brows.

"Tell them what you told me about Costa Rica, Hay."

Hayward Lugo studied her. "What."

"You know, the monkeys. At the hotel."

He examined her a millisecond longer and made a small, unreadable gesture.

"You can have your own monkey," he said at last. "If you want one."

Cissy Lugo blinked at her husband, a few longer hairs from her bangs catching in her thickly mascaraed lashes and moving in unison with her eyelids.

Hilda broke the silence. "That's a beautiful piano. Do you play?"

"Nobody in the house plays, nor does friend or family," Hayward Lugo said. "But we don't so much *live* in rooms as visit them."

Proudhorse said, "We have just a few questions—"

Cissy Lugo said, "My friends tell me Costa Rica has a lot of jade. Jade like you wouldn't believe."

She picked up a long, thin knife with a pearlized handle and a sharp-tined fork at the end of its blade and thrust it toward Proudhorse, who shrank back in surprise.

"Did you know there are different colors of jade?" she continued, unaware of Proudhorse's reaction—or the reaction of the others, rapt by the progress of the knife

93

blade toward Proudhorse's heart. "Which is pretty weird considering *jade* is another word for green."

She dive-bombed the knife abruptly, speared an errant hunk of lox lying on the polished tabletop in front of Proudhorse, and flicked the lox onto her plate with a lacquered fingernail.

"I mean *pink* jade," she said with a shrug that lifted her large breasts dramatically. "What's *that* about?"

Hayward Lugo produced a burst of mirthless laughter.

Ben now saw Cissy reaching toward Joe Proudhorse again, this time holding a large linen napkin. As if planning to wipe his nose, Ben thought.

Proudhorse drew back again, bassett eyes wary.

"But of course there's always the rain forest," Cissy said. She rubbed the napkin over the tabletop in front of Proudhorse, where the wayward lox had left a smear of grease, and retired the napkin to her lap.

"What do you think?" she asked, looking at them expectantly.

Hilda and Proudhorse exchanged glances, and Ben realized they'd been so engaged in the dumb-show of knife, lox, and napkin that not one of them had followed the thread of Cissy Lugo's conversation.

"Sorry," Hilda said. "Could you repeat that, please?"

"What?" Cissy asked. "*All* of it?"

Hayward Lugo gave another bark of laughter, upended his glass, and tongued an olive into his mouth.

"Tell us—" Proudhorse began.

"Toby's problem, Cecilia," Lugo said.

"Hayward!"

"They'll find out soon enough. They *are* police, ma petite chou. And since, thanks to you, everyone knows anyway."

He turned to the detectives. "My son has . . . *had* . . . a gambling addiction."

"He *gambled*," Cissy put in.

"He was an addict," Lugo interjected. "I've bailed him out thousands of times."

"Thousands. Oh, please."

"I recently cut him off," he told the detectives. "Said he'd have to find his way out of this by himself and—"

"With the result that he was murdered, thanks to—"

He looked menacing. "Don't say it."

"Shreveport will be after *us* next," she muttered into her glass.

"What, you think Shreveport put out a contract or something? Stupid! Why not all of Las Vegas?"

"Don't be a complete ass, Hay."

"Don't be a complete fool, Cecilia."

"Don't be a complete—"

He cut her off with a roll of small gray eyes.

Proudhorse started to speak, but Ben held up a hand of restraint.

"Talk to Toby's bookie," Hayward Lugo told the detectives.

"Hay. For Christ's sake."

"Who is?" Proudhorse asked.

"Beats the hell out of me," Lugo said. "Ask his friends."

"He doesn't have any friends," said Cissy. "*Didn't* have friends, I mean. He had enemies. Including his family."

Lugo muttered something Ben didn't catch.

"Does the name Zack Ruben mean anything to either of you?" Hilda asked.

No.

"Lulu Ruben?"

No.

"Jiggy Ruben?"

Cissy Lugo's eyes flickered.

Ben straightened.

"Jeremiah Ruben?" he put in. "Jiggy."

Both faces closed.

"Where were you on August 13?" Proudhorse asked. "And on August 6 and 20?"

Cissy Lugo, in transit to the kitchen, stopped as if stuck with a needle.

Hayward Lugo said, "He was our *son*, you mean bastards. We may have been piss-poor parents, but—"

"To answer the question—" Ben said.

"Where was I? I was in my office until late. Till midnight, anyway. I often work late. Cissy was here. I don't know what those other dates are about. I'd have to check my calendar."

Cissy nodded vigorously.

"I'll give you some names," Lugo said. "As it happens, I do know Toby's bookie. Name's Lacefield. "

Ben looked up from his notebook. "Lonnie Lacefield?"

Lugo looked startled. Hilda and Proudhorse looked interested. And Cissy looked like she wanted to hiss.

"Don't forget LeRoy," she said. "I think those two work together. LeRoy Shatto and Lonnie Lacefield. Trudelle Williams. She was the girl—"

"Oh, for Christ's sake, Cecilia." Lugo turned to Ben. "Trudelle's an old high school friend of Toby's. Just a friend."

"Didn't they say they wanted the names of friends?" Cissy called, in the kitchen now and raising her voice above the sound of running water.

"Let me ask again about Jiggy Ruben," Ben said, raising his own voice so she could hear him.

She came back from the kitchen with a fresh Bloody Mary and waved a celery stick as if preparing to speak.

But Hayward Lugo stared hard at his wife, and she bit off the end of the celery stick with a crunch and said nothing.

"I'll give you the names you need," Lugo said.

#

Outside, Hilda grinned at Proudhorse.

"I thought Cissy Lugo was going after you with that knife."

"She was just using it to cut the tension."

"You went all grumpy-looking when she explained that *jade* meant green."

"Hmf."

"And Lugo. He calls Cissy his little shoe? What's that about?"

"Ma petite chou," Ben said. "French for *my little cabbage.*"

Hilda snorted. "You check out that piano?"

Ben nodded. The Lugos' grand piano, the size and shine and majesty of it . . . He had seen its like before—in the Blum brothers' apartment.

"You still play?" Hilda asked.

"Not much," he said. "Proudhorse plays."

She gave her partner a look that screwed up both her eyes and her mouth at once.

"You're kidding."

97

Proudhorse cast his solemn glance her way. "Why's that so surprising?"

"I guess I don't see a grand piano on a reservation."

Proudhorse shot up a burst of uncharacteristic laughter, the copper skin around his mournful eyes crinkling.

"You think I lived in a teepee? Hi! Ni! Yah!"

CHAPTER SEVENTEEN

Wednesday evening, August 22

Ben was fixing dinner when Andrew called.

"Hey, bud," Ben said. "Where are you?"

"*Where am I?*"

Ben laughed.

"Library," Andrew said. "Handlers on a break. What's going on?"

Ben told him.

"Here's my thinking, Andrew. What if it's not a true serial? What if the killer wants us to think the killings are random—when they're really a ruse to cover motive and connection to the so-called real murder."

"You have a reason to say this?"

"A feeling."

"Oh. That." Andrew said. "So which is the so-called *real* victim? Or victims? The last?"

"Maybe not, if the killer's as smart as I think he is. Buried—so to speak—in the middle? Bood, stop that."

"How's the Boodleman?"

"Bood's good. Underfoot, complaining that he's hungry."

Bood shoved his nose against Ben's calf, and Ben offered him a sprig of parsley. The dog eyed it with suspicion but took it into his mouth tentatively, shifted it from cheek to cheek delicately with shriveled lips, and spat it on the floor.

"But wait, Andrew."

He told him about Zack Ruben's watch and his uncle Jiggy.

"This Jiggy's still—maybe just two-bit enterprise, I don't know. I'm guessing he started young, with neighborhood theft. He's tight with a couple bookies named LeRoy Shatto and Lonnie Lacefield. So gambling for sure and maybe more, maybe drugs."

"And maybe got away with murder a couple of decades ago."

"I'm putting Malone on it. Although he doesn't know it yet. He'll piss and moan, but I have my hands full, and maybe we can get Jacko to revisit his bulldog days."

"Malone himself being bent and all."

"And maybe you can network with some guys who were active in the D-FW area."

He repeated the trio's names—Ruben, Shatto, Lacefield.

"The only other new bit is—"

He told him about the notes on his windshield.

"Forensics agrees they've nothing in common with the murder notes. Computer generated, garden-variety stock. The murder notes are hand-printed, black marker, heavy stock."

"What do these other notes say again?"

"Clueless, aren't you. Poor little rich boy. Running out of luck, rich boy. That kind of thing."

"Who's jealous of you, Ben? Besides everybody?"

They were both thinking the same thing, but Andrew said it: *Jack Malone.*

"Jack's a wreck, but he's not a sneak. And he's not long on stealth or finesse. A note on a windshield? I'm not sure. A *sledgehammer* on a windshield? Now you're talking."

"Bottom line: No suspects."

"Right. But it's early days. We have to revisit everyone in the earlier cases, and we haven't done in-depths for Daniel/Craven."

"Any alibi problems so far?"

"*Alibi!*"

"Huh?"

"Hang on." Ben grabbed the crossword puzzle from the kitchen island, where he'd tossed it the night before. "What do you want to bet, Andrew, that *alibi* means *elsewhere* in Latin?"

The shift in topic would have been too much for anyone but Andrew. He hesitated only a moment before he said: "How many letters?"

"Five." Ben located *ammoniate*, which he'd penned in the night before, and used its "A" to print *alibi* into the five small spaces of One Down.

"OK, Andrew, that L on *alibi*. Five letters. Offspring of lion and tiger."

"Liger," Andrew said immediately.

Ben laughed. "I'd say why didn't I think of that, but I *did*. And thought it was ridiculous."

"I'm serious. Look it up."

Liger. Ben laughed again. No shit.

"OK, the I on *liger*. Seven letters meaning accuse."

They said the word in unison.

"Now we're cooking." Ben printed *impeach* in the little squares and examined the Down clues. "Next, six letters, starts with B, goes with *wire* or *words*."

"Barbed."

"Right down your alley. Last one. Eight letters. Means cash-strapped—oh, yeah—*illiquid*."

Ben scribbled in the word and slapped the newspaper onto the island.

"OK, bro. Maybe we didn't get far with the case, but at least we conquered one quadrant of a crossword."

CHAPTER EIGHTEEN

Thursday morning, August 23

Ben entered the conference room briskly and took a seat. Everybody back in place. Except Malone.

"Some interesting stuff from the Lugos—Proudhorse and Hilda will fill you in. For the rest, we've had twenty-four hours to ponder, so let's talk."

Joe Proudhorse broke their silence.

"Cyberman copies sensational murders from the Net."

"And that gets us . . ."

"In deep shit," said Malone from the doorway. He came in and pulled out a chair at the far end of the table, away from the others, who were bunched at the other end. He slapped down his notebook and sat with a grunt, his chair still back from the table, then pulled out his large handkerchief and blew his nose.

"Fuckin' flu," he said.

Everyone looked at Ben.

"We were saying: Cyberman is copying sensational murders from the Internet. And that gets us where?"

Hilda shoved the box of pastries she'd brought to the center of the conference table.

"First," she said, "what does it *mean*?"

Chief Saenz entered the room in a cloud of aftershave, his hair morning damp and shining like coal, and took a seat against the window.

"What does it mean, and how does he choose?" Ben said. "He's surfing the Net—is he looking for a victim he likes? Or an M.O. he likes?"

"The M.O.s are nothing alike," Kenechi put in.

"Victim, then."

"Those aren't anything alike, either."

Chief Saenz rose and examined the box of pastries, found a chocolate-filled bun and sat back down, backlit by the window, his face in shadow against the blinds.

"So we have, first, a toddler," Ben said. "Second, a grad student. Third, a priest and a parishioner. What links them? Besides the Internet. And the fact that they're the victims of a serial killer."

The only sound in the room was Malone's rhythmic wheeze, like a spent accordion.

"OK," Ben said. "If there are links, we haven't found them. What else can we say about the vics?"

"They get older," Pratt said. "A three-year-old. A guy in his twenties. Two middle-aged victims."

"A single, single, and a double," Naldo added.

Proudhorse looked at them from across the table, forehead creased. "So . . . A senior citizen? A triple?"

"Ah, cripes," said Hilda.

"Does Cyberman choose the case," Ben asked, "then find a victim who matches? Or does he already have the victim in mind?"

"If he already has the victim in mind, that's not random." Kenechi said.

"Damn straight."

"Say there's some people I want dead—a baby, a student, a priest." Hilda asked. "What's that about?"

"Doesn't have to make sense," Proudhorse said.

"I'd say case first," said Pratt.

"Why?" Ben asked.

"I don't know."

Everyone laughed. Except Malone, who sat wheezing, eyes downcast.

"Seems more logical," Pratt said.

"To *you*," Proudhorse said.

Ben chewed his lip. "You find a cyberspace case you like, something sensational. Something notorious and accessible. It involves a toddler, so you find a toddler. You begin there."

"What if these aren't real *serials*?" Kenechi asked.

Ben nodded encouragement.

"Different killers?" Hilda said. "We've got the notes."

"No. I mean what if the killings aren't random. They're with deliberation rather than compulsion. He has one target. The others are red herrings."

Ben nodded again. "Go on."

"The killer has one intended victim, the others are smokescreen. When he gets his target, the killings will stop."

"Why?"

Kenechi turned his pen end-for-end in his big hands. "The link between killer and target is too obvious?"

"Let's follow that."

"If the killer murders his target, suspicion will immediately fall on him. So he develops this serial ruse to muddy the waters, to hide his connection to the victim."

"Lugo," said Hilda.

Everyone looked at her.

"Case One is a toddler in both the original case and the copycat case." She said. "Case Three is an Episcopal priest and a parishioner in both the original and the copycat case. Toby Lugo is the odd man out. No grad student in the original case."

"So you're thinking the grad student isn't dictated by the original case, so the grad student must be killer's choice?"

"In New Orleans, the victims ran the gamut," said Naldo.

"Not quite," Ben said. "Most of the Axeman's vics were Italian grocers."

"But not all," Pratt said.

"Some just in the wrong place at the wrong time," Naldo added.

"But even supposing they *were* all grocers—I mean *especially* supposing," Hilda said. "Lugo's still the odd man out."

"OK, let's say Lugo," Ben said. "Cases One and Three smokescreen, Lugo sandwiched between. To hide him?"

Malone spoke from his distant spot at the table. "I don't like Lugo for it."

"Why?" Ben asked.

"Yeah, *why*. That's what I mean. Killer couldn't find a grad student case to copy?"

Hilda looked disgruntled. "But doesn't that strengthen Lugo as target? Not perfect but the best the killer could do?"

"Ay," said Rolando Saenz from his seat by the window. "My head's startin' to hurt."

Everyone but Ben looked at the chief, sitting against the window, but he didn't say anything more, just sat against the blinds, a faceless presence, hair backlit and shining like raven feathers.

Ben studied Malone, who leaned back, legs crossed, one pantleg hitched to show a hairless expanse of calf. His notebook was open on his knee, pages blank.

"Who *do* you like, Jack?" Ben asked.

"If there *is* a single target." Malone uncrossed his legs and sat straighter. "I think it's just a sicko serial. Straightforward."

"If Lugo was the target and the other murders smokescreen," Proudhorse said, "and Cyberman's not a sicko serialist, then he's done killing, no?"

"And if he is a sicko serialist," Malone responded, "and Lugo wasn't the target, then he's not done killing."

Ben groaned and sat back in his chair.

"Not necessarily," Kenechi said.

"Ay yi yi." The chief got up, turning at the door to glare at them. "Let's just hope to hell he *is* done." He punctuated the air with a fragment of chocolate bun. "Or that we stop him before he finishes. And that we don't get any more notes. Ben? Can I see you when you're through?"

Everyone sat in silence when the door closed on the chief, Ben doodling, Kenechi brooding, Hilda fidgeting, Proudhorse squinting at the ceiling, Pratt and Naldo frowning, Malone breathing—in, out, in . . . .

"You looking into Jiggy Ruben, Jack?" Ben asked without looking up from his doodles.

"I don't see anything there," Malone said.

"Whatcha got so far?"

"He runs a vintage car operation near Midlothian."

"What kind of operation?"

"Seems legit. Warehouses vintage cars. Called Jeremiah's Auto Stable."

Ben sketched a high-roofed Ford Model T. Put some tires on it. "Is there a living in that?"

"Vintage cars?" Hilda put in. "You kidding? We're talking real money. I just read about a '70 Superbird Hemi that brought 150K at an auction."

"I mean is there a living in warehousing them?"

"These collectors are fanatics about their cars," Malone said, his hand straying toward his breast pocket for a cigarette, straying away again. "Jiggy Ruben not only houses them, he keeps them in mint condition. Owners come out and drive them around his paved track. Or his staff does." Phlegm roughened his voice, and he coughed into his fist. "The cars are on call twenty-four-seven to the owners—waxed, gassed, and ready to go." He coughed into his fist again. "The cars, not the owners."

"I can see why they call it a stable," Ben said. "You don't think it's a front?"

"Like I said."

"You talk to him?"

"Not yet."

"Find any Blum brother connections?"

Malone pursed his lips and blew. "Not yet."

"When?"

Malone's eyes were hard.

"Soon as I can."

Ben let a couple seconds tick by, then turned to Proudhorse and Hilda.

"You finish your report on the Lugo interview?"

Proudhorse pushed a short pile of printouts toward Ben, who dismantled the pile and looked at his watch.

"I need to see what the chief wants."

He slid copies of Hilda and Proudhorse's report across the table to the other detectives. "Read this. We'll talk again at the end of the day. Meantime—"

He turned to Proudhorse. "We need the priest's backstory. Can you get that together?"

"It's all but done."

"Good. Gaylord Daniel would have been fifty at his next birthday, and he was at All Saints for fifteen years. Meaning he came in his mid-thirties. Where was he before that? And was Claire Craven his first dalliance with a parishioner? We need an accounting of his life not only at All Saints, but at his former churches."

Joe Proudhorse filled a page in his notebook with big black scrawl as Ben spoke, and Ben made a snap decision. He'd give All Saints to Proudhorse—they'd be no match for his dark Comanche stare.

"Duff Craven mentioned a parishioner named Verlie Mae Cheek. Called her the congregation rumormonger. You and Hilda go talk to her asap. Parish gossip, troublemaker, whatever, she might have some inside info."

He pushed his chair back from the table, but didn't get up.

"Pratt. Naldo. Get Jiggy Ruben in here for an interview asap. Let me know if you have any trouble with him. Meantime, scope out his auto stable. Talk to whoever's there, but don't show any cards." He turned to Malone. "That OK with you, Jack?"

Ben looked around the table—Proudhorse and Hilda already out of their chairs, Pratt and Naldo pushing back from the table. "For now, our focus will be Toby Lugo. Treat him as the target, the odd man out, as Hilda said. Keep looking for connections between the vics. Anything, no matter how small."

They filed out, Hilda looking pleased, Malone rising.

"Hang on a minute, Jack," Ben said.

Malone eased back in his chair, eyes wary, both men sitting well back from the table, plenty of distance between them.

"Couple names I want to try out on you," Ben said. "First, though—would you rather have the Craven piece of this case?"

Malone looked blank. "What do you mean? Didn't you just give that to Proudhorse?"

"I gave him Gaylord Daniel. We're working four vics on the serial, four cases. Daniel's just one."

Jack looked petulant. "Wasn't I checking out your cold case? The Blum murders?"

High maintenance! For effect, Ben tore dramatically at his heavy black hair. But if he was seeking effect, he got none. Malone simply pulled his wadded handkerchief from his pocket without changing his expression and swiped at his nose.

"You seemed lukewarm," Ben said. "I thought you might want something besides your same ol' same ol'."

"Not to say *why me*, but why me? Churchy types? What do I know about them? Same ol' same ol' doesn't bother me. Street people, druggies, petty criminals . . . that doesn't scare me." He grin was more of a rictus. "Least not as much as church folks and Jesus freaks."

"Fine," Ben said without looking up from his notebook and his Model T sketch. "We set up a meeting with All Saints' secretary and music director. Kenechi and I will go." Ben paused to add some finishing touches to his Model T. "Those names . . . LeRoy Shatto and Lonnie Lacefield. Mean anything?"

Malone shrugged.

"Shatto. With a T."

Malone hitched his beefy shoulders again. "Shatto. A bookie. So's Lacefield, yeah. Weird dude. Wears Indian clothes. Not an Indian, though, no way."

Ben thought of the blond ponytail, the fringed jacket, the moccasins.

"Jiggy Ruben. You run across him before?"

Malone hesitated a millisecond. "Somewhere along the line."

Ben looked up from his sketch and met his partner's eyes—small and pink-rimmed, like a pig's. They collided with Ben's for a second and slid away.

"What do you know about him?"

"For sure? What I've told you. Not that there isn't plenty more. I used to have a good woods animal nose. Could smell danger. Not so good anymore, but I still get a whiff time to time."

Ben stifled the impulse to suggest what might have ruined Malone's nose.

"You get a whiff from Jiggy Ruben?"

"More than a whiff. He's bad news."

"Call what I got a hunch." Ben kept his gaze steady on Malone. "Gambling for sure. And maybe trafficking." He paused for emphasis. "But I don't want to go missing the drugs if they're there." He paused again. "I also don't want the drugs to go missing."

Malone took a moment to read his face and words and red spread across his cheeks like a brushfire. He turned toward the door.

"Keep me posted," Ben said.

"Fuck yourself," Malone said without turning around.

A lot can happen in the space of a synapse, in the time it takes for one nerve cell to connect with another. Ben's intention, and habit, was to ignore Malone, to refuse to rise to his bait—to tear the sketch from his notebook, ball it up, overhand it into the wastebasket, dismiss Malone with no show of emotion.

Ben's high road.

But what he saw in that tiny tick of time was that Malone understood his aversion to disorder and public show, and was manipulating it. And in that fragment of a second, before he could stop himself, he bounded around the conference table, grabbed Malone by the shirt, jerked him around, and put everything he had into a haymaker that smeared Malone's nose toward his right cheekbone— obliquely but still with a satisfying crunch of cartilage. Because Malone twisted at a critical instant, Ben's fist flattened his nose in transit and, still flying, struck the window of the conference room door. The glass shattered, stopping Ben's punch with one clean, deep cut across his knuckles.

What he'd remember later: the chief's fury and Kenechi's calm. Hilda round-eyed. Pratt and Naldo and Sly hovering, astonished. The rest of the squad room ready to snicker as soon as the coast was clear. Ben and Kenechi leaving for the ER, the cut on Ben's hand seeping blood through a towel from the break room, darkening the platinum gray of his shirt cuff, staining the red silk of his tie and the lap of his charcoal trousers. Everyone looking at the mess as though they didn't see enough of it on the job. Blood. Ungovernable. Indelible. A saturated pigment—causing a visceral, primal reaction. You could almost get the same reaction, Ben thought, by mixing a little of the strongest crimson or scarlet on the palette and daubing it on the canvas.

And, as he and Kenechi left for the ER, here was Malone, sopping at his nose, his own geyser of blood, shoving a hand at Ben as he passed. Wanting to shake! The code. After goading Ben into that disgraceful little vignette—not that it was Malone's fault, no fucking way—Malone offering his hand not in shame but with some sort of congratulatory pride that sickened Ben. And that respect or kinship or whatever it was kindling in Malone's eyes. Ben saw it on the faces of some others in the squad room, too. Blood brothers in their aggression and loss of control. Man up! What utter bullshit. Fucking primitive schoolyard shit, bullies and the bully's code.

As Nell would say, the antithesis of the highly evolved.

And count me among them, he thought, self-disgust clogging his throat.

Ben slapped Malone's hand away. And saw his colleagues' frowns of disapproval before he and Kenechi went out the door.

Not adhering to the code.

Fine. In Malone's words, fuck 'em.

#

"This isn't necessarily a bad thing," Kenechi said on the short drive to the hospital, reacting to Ben's grim silence.

"Bullshit," Ben said immediately. "It's a fucking disgrace, and you know it. It's everything I hate."

"Lets them know you're human."

"Was there any doubt?"

"Maybe."

Ben made a disgusted sound. "Yeah, let's get together and feel all right. Display our flaws so we can forgive them. Sing a little Bob Marley."

Kenechi was silent, and Ben perversely decided to say more.

113

"And I hope you don't mistake self-hatred for arrogance."
Kenechi's small smile was inscrutable. "I don't."

CHAPTER NINETEEN

Midmorning Thursday, August 23

"Women at All Saints were jealous of Claire. They thought Duff doted on her because he always put one of his red roses beside her plate at the church suppers," said Regina Tupp, church secretary.

"Who, exactly?" Ben asked.

"Verlie Mae Cheek, for one," said Lily Tansy, music director.

Ben looked at them with interest, then thumbed back through his notebook to Duff Craven's interview.

My wife hated roses, especially red roses.

Ben, Kenechi, and Hilda were in All Saints' chamber-like offices—Hilda in case the misses Tupp and Tansy were more comfortable with a woman. An unnecessary concern, Ben saw. The detectives had mounted the stone steps to the side door—which again squealed like a pulled nail—and now were settled with frosty glasses of sweet ice tea and flowered plates full of gingersnaps.

The ladies, side by side on the sofa, regarded Ben with curiosity as he reached into his pocket with his bandaged hand and withdrew his pen.

"What happened to your hand?" asked Lily.

Ben ignored the question. He found he could prop his pen against his bandage and otherwise hold it in its usual position between index and middle fingers. He felt harried and irritable—the confrontation with Malone, the rushed trip to the ER, the hurried change from his bloody clothing to the clean clothing Kenechi fetched from his place.

And now tea and cookies with church ladies.

"You mentioned Verlie Mae Cheek," he said.

"And her husband, John," said Regina. "Pillars of the church."

"Now, Reg," murmured Lily.

Ben looked up from his notebook.

"It's true. The two of them, so full of spite. Feeding one another's self-righteousness."

"Well, I don't know," said Lily.

"Yes, you do."

"You said Verlie Mae was jealous of Claire Craven," Ben said. "What made her jealous?"

"Everything. There was a time when John Cheek hung around Claire like she was a bitch in heat—"

"Oh, my," said Lily.

"But not lately," Regina added.

"Lately?"

"Lately, John had it in for Claire."

"Why's that?"

"All I know is this. I came into the community room, and Claire and John were in the kitchen quarreling. Screaming at each other, more like. I called out a halooo and banged the door, and they stopped."

"What were they saying?"

"What I heard Claire say was *if you weren't such a hypocrite, it wouldn't matter.*

"Do you have any idea what she was talking about?"

Regina looked at him steadily for a millisecond.

"I guess I thought she was talking about John Cheek being such a hypocrite."

Lily gave a whoop of laughter, and Ben stifled his own smile.

"What time," he addressed both women, "did you leave All Saints Sunday night after the church supper? I'd like each of you to respond, please."

They stared at him, slowly grasping the import of the question.

"Oh, my god," Lily breathed, and Regina raised a liver-spotted hand to her throat.

An image flashed through Ben's mind. The misses Tansy and Tupp in their summer dresses—fragile, snowy-haired Lily, bent under the weight of ancestral jewelry, smelling like the flower that named her, and bespectacled Regina, blinking rapidly above rouged cheeks, improbable burgundy tendrils trembling beneath her purple turban. The two of them. Strangling a baby. Wielding an ax in the night. Shooting a priest.

Ben again hid his amusement. But Kenechi didn't. He tossed back his head and threw a high-pitched guffaw at the ceiling, his upper molars glinting gold. Instantly recovering, he raised a pale palm in apology.

"You're not suspects, ladies," Ben said. "We're trying to verify some times."

"Oh." Regina blinked at them through her thick lenses. "We left the supper by nine-thirty, I should think. I went upstairs and collected some work I'd left on the church computer and was home for the ten o'clock news."

"Yes," Lily said.

Kenechi turned to Regina. "You said a lot of people at All Saints thought Duff doted on Claire, Miss Tupp," he said. "Did you have reason to think otherwise?"

Regina hesitated.

"This isn't gossip, Reg," Lily said. "It's the *police*."

Lily turned to Ben. "If Duff Craven doted on Claire, we never saw it. Maybe it's just the way some men treat their wives in public—and I don't know how he treated her when they were alone. But I don't think he was kind to her."

She stood cross-armed and pinch-lipped, prepared to stand by her words.

"Can you be more specific?" Ben asked.

"Once I made a soufflé for our Sunday night supper, and Claire said she felt like she was in Gay Paree. And Duff said, *I wish you were.*"

"Tell them about the time he turned the table over," Regina prodded.

Lily stopped her with a crooked, jewel-laden finger. "Another time—this was at a church supper, too—someone mentioned Italy, and she said she'd like to live in Tuscany. And Duff said, *why don't you?* That's what I mean."

"Tell them about the table," Regina said.

"How did she respond?" Ben asked Lily.

"She usually made a joke. Or ignored him. That time, though, she said, 'Duff secretly hates me.' And he said, *it's no secret.*"

Regina clucked again. "I'm sick and tired of being Christian about things like that," she said. "Duff Craven's a bastard."

Lily put her hand over her mouth.

"*Bastard,*" she said again, with a toss of her turbaned head. "I didn't tell you, Lily, but I heard Claire on the phone in the office. Couple weeks ago. I came in from the sanctuary, not through that noisy back door—" She broke off.

Lily said, "Well, go on, Reg, now you've started."

"She said she felt she were turning to stone, like that mother in mythology whose children died. She said the mother's name, but—"

"Niobe?" Kenechi put in.

Regina blinked. "Yes! That's what she said. Niobe."

"Niobe," Lily said. "Is she famous?"

"Go on, Miss Tupp," Ben said.

"Is she in the bible?" Lily asked.

"How did you kow that?" Regina asked Kenechi.

"I'm a detective," Kenechi said. "I know everything."

"Go on, Miss Tupp," Ben said again. "What else did you hear?"

"She said she couldn't bear it, that he had been watching her, that he even followed her. She said she had to get away. And she said a lot more, but it was a jumble because she was crying hard by then."

"Who was she talking about?"

Regina looked at Ben as if at a backward child. "Duff?"

"But you don't know that, do you," Lily said. "Hearsay, right, detective?"

Regina sighed. "Oh, please."

"Not exactly," Ben said.

"Do you know who she was talking to?" Hilda asked.

"No, not hearsay," Lily said. "Speculation. Right?"

Regina looked at Hilda. "I guess I supposed it was Father Daniel."

"Speculation," Lily repeated.

"*Was* it Father Daniel?" Regina said to the detectives. "I don't know. And if it was, did she tell him because he was her priest, or because he was her lover? I don't know that either. But I can tell you this, detectives." She regarded them a moment longer, her eyes magnified by her thick lenses. "My heart went out to her."

"You said Duff turned the table over?" Kenechi asked.

"He did."

"What do you mean?"

Regina made an exasperated sound. "What do I *mean*? What do *you* mean, what do I mean? He turned the table over."

"Long time ago," Lily said.

"It still happened."

"What table? Why?" Ben asked.

Lily answered. "The church supper table. When we were cleaning up. Peas and baked beans and ham and escalloped potatoes and dinner rolls all over—"

"They don't need to know that part, Lily," Regina said.

"When? Why did he do this?"

"He was furious because—" Lily broke off at her friend's expression.

"That really *is* gossip, Lily," Regina said and turned to Ben. "We don't want to talk about this. Verlie Mae. She's the one who knows about it. Or pretends to."

"And doesn't mind talking about it. She even told—"

"Lily," Regina said.

The detectives waited, but the women were now united, arms crossed, faces closed.

Ben sighed.

"Do you have a church directory we could take with us?"

"And could we take a look at the sanctuary?" Hilda asked.

"Oh, yes!" Lily said, beaming. She took Hilda's arm and drew her close.

"Are you a lesbian?" she whispered.

120

"Who wants to know?" Hilda whispered back.

"I probably seem indiscreet—" the older woman said.

"No kidding."

"But we don't have any lesbians in the congregation."

"That you know of," Hilda put in.

"And I just thought it would be nice if—"

"I'll keep it in mind," Hilda said.

They stepped through a tall arch into All Saints' hush and gloom, the stained air in the nave scented with incense and candle wax. Beyond the chancel, the apse was in twilight, the altar unlit beneath a trio of stained glass windows. Ben moved to the back of the empty church for a moment to view the arched ceiling and rough-hewn beams. The lofty sanctuary with its space and silence and blood reds and dark woods reminded him of an interior by a Dutch master. After a moment, he strode down the center aisle, shoes silent on the red carpeting, and stopped beneath the stained glass windows above the altar. He found the images rustic and somber: An angel speaking to a man in a flowing beard. The bearded man brandishing a dagger over a reclining boy. The angel restraining the bearded man and offering him a ram to sacrifice instead.

"Abraham and Isaac," Hilda said at his shoulder.

"Just another irrational demand from our loving father," said a voice behind them.

Duff Craven stood in the aisle in his gray workclothes and dirty chamois gloves, a lethal-looking gardening implement with three sharp tines gripped like a weapon in one hand.

#

They left All Saints on the sprint, Kenechi saying he was late for a meeting, he and Ben walking so fast across the churchyard that Hilda had to jog to keep up. Ben put the unmarked in reverse, lurched backward then forward, and left the lot, throwing a little gravel.

The radio crackled and Sly's voice came on. Where were they and how soon were they coming in? Chief's antsy. Akundi's late for their meeting. Ben glanced at Kenechi, who dropped his eyes. His meeting was with the *chief?*

"And Proudhorse is going apeshit, too," Sly added.

"Proudhorse? Why?"

"I don't know. Some stuff he dug up about one of the vics in the churchyard. That priest."

CHAPTER TWENTY

Thursday afternoon, August 23

Ben entered the squad room behind Kenechi, who hustled toward the chief's office, and Hilda stayed hard on Ben's heels as far as his office door.

"Got a minute? I've been wanting to ask you something."

"Want to step inside?" Ben asked.

She saw Proudhorse approaching and dismissed Ben's offer with a wave of her stubby hand.

"No, that's all right. It's—it's Kenechi," she said quickly. "Not that it's any of my business, but is he OK?"

"Ken? Yes. I mean I think so. Why?"

"He seems, I don't know, preoccupied or worried or something."

"He gets that way on a case, Hilda."

"I mean unusually so. You haven't noticed?"

He'd noticed.

"I just—" Without finishing her thought, Hilda veered off toward the Ladies' room.

Proudhorse came down the corridor, car keys in his hand.

"Got the scoop on Father Daniel, but I need to leave now to see that Verlie Mae Cheek."

Ben nodded. "Got time for a thumbnail?"

"You were right, plenty of history there. Gaylord Daniel couldn't keep it zipped. One of his lovers killed herself."

Ben rubbed his jaw. "If I'm gone when you get back, call me at home tonight, OK?"

Hilda swung through the door of the Ladies', drying her hands on a paper towel, and Joe hustled her down the corridor.

#

Ben stood for a second outside the chief's office. Inside, Saenz's blinds were partially drawn against the afternoon sun, but the slats let in knife-thin blades of yellow light that cut everything they fell upon into slices, like an Escher drawing. Ben saw Kenechi and Saenz on opposite sides of the chief's desk, looking serious, the chief listening, nodding.

He went back to his office and kept one eye on the corridor. When Kenechi strode past, Ben went to the window overlooking the squad room. Kenechi sat with his back to Ben, intermittently writing something on a notepad, but mostly staring at nothing, his big hands loose on the desktop.

This was what Hilda was talking about. He stepped behind his desk and picked up the phone, stood with his index finger poised to dial, changed his mind, set the phone in its base, and went into the corridor.

Chief Saenz was still behind his desk, rummaging through a box of chocolates. The door was ajar, and Ben rapped at the casing. The chief motioned him in.

Ben took the deep leather chair that Kenechi had just vacated and said, "I'm curious about something . . . well, concerned."

Saenz stopped chewing and looked wary.

"It's Ken Akundi," Ben said. "Something's wrong. Maybe it's none of my business, and you could tell me that. But . . . maybe it is my business. So I'm asking."

The chief rustled through the empty wrappers in the candy box and popped another chocolate into his mouth. "It's your business—he's on your team."

Ben waited.

"Keep this to yourself. Grace is pregnant. He's quitting the force."

The air went out of Ben, as if he'd been punched. The last thing he expected.

"Grace wants to give up her job," Saenz continued, "until the baby's in pre-school or kindergarten. It's what she did with James and Amy, and it's what she wants to do now."

"I still don't see why—"

Saenz waved a hand impatiently, as if batting at a fly. "Ben. Your momma's rich."

In the silence that followed, Ben half expected him to add: *And your pa is good lookin'.*

Instead, he said, "Maybe you don't even realize how underpaid cops are."

Ben crossed and uncrossed his legs.

"Ken might not like my telling this," the chief said. "Grace had a small inheritance from her grandparents, but that's gone. And they've done OK on two paychecks. But they also send money to Ken's relatives in Nigeria. Now—"

"Jesus Christ. He's one of the best detectives I know."

"Yep." Saenz spoke with the air of One Who Faces Facts. "No doubt about it."

"Pay him more," Ben said, knowing instantly how naïve that sounded.

The chief looked at him out of the tops of his eyes and didn't bother to respond.

"What's he going to do?" Ben asked.

"Return to academe."

Ben raised his brows. "Like teachers aren't underpaid?"

"Professors make a decent living. And deans and department heads can make good money, depending on the school. Kenechi has a Ph.D, remember. Like you. But unlike you, he doesn't have a trust fund."

Saenz pushed back his swivel chair and rose.

Ben stood, too, flexing his knees.

"He's had a couple offers," Saenz added.

"Shit. Where?"

Saenz shrugged. "Out of state's all I know. But he doesn't want to move unless he has to."

Kenechi's doctorate was in chemical engineering so, likely, engineering school somewhere. Ben knew how marketable Ken would be in academe—a scholarly émigré, an established man of color.

"Shit, shit, shit," he said.

Back in his office, he again looked through the glass at Kenechi, sitting in his cubicle in the squad room, his wiry salt-and-pepper head moving side to side as he sifted through a file of folders. Ben studied his own office, the institutional gray-green walls, the no-color carpeting, the modest faux wood-grain furniture and file cabinets. The best the department could afford. He wondered what it would be like not to be able to do what he believed in because he couldn't make a living doing it.

And for the zillionth time, he felt the shortcomings of fortune—first, how it set him apart. And second, how it did not settle the ills of the earth. He'd watched his mother throw money at problems. And still, her son was in prison. And still, the poor—her constant concern—were poor.

Money helped only as long as it lasted.

His immediate impulse was to trump up some ruse by which he could pay a boost in Ken's salary on the QT. He wasn't his mother's son for nothing. And he knew not only how ridiculous that was, but also that no one would allow it. He'd fought that sort of impulse before. The ultimate insult. Getting in the way of people finding their own answers.

And he was sorry Kenechi hadn't come to him. But he knew why he hadn't and that he'd talk to Ben only when his future was settled. Kenechi was proud. The only reason he went to the chief was that he had to—he was seeking other work and protocol demanded it.

He looked through the glass at Kenechi Akundi's broad back and was surprised at the depth of what he felt. And what he felt was loss.

CHAPTER TWENTY-ONE

Thursday evening, August 23

Ben didn't get away from the office until late and, mindful of his bandaged hand, stopped at a Chinese buffet for some take-out. The food was not very good, but the place was on the way, and the shells-on steamed shrimp were edible.

He piled one section of his Styrofoam container full of the shellfish, added a little tub of red sauce and some lemon wedges, and cruised along the buffet offerings, which he knew from experience were such a marvel of tastelessness that he wondered how the chef achieved it. He took a generous scoop of steamed rice—could you ruin rice?—and a few nuggets of orange chicken. He remembered he had a half-bottle of cab left over from last night and a fresh loaf of chewy whole-grain bread from La Madeleine.

He garnished his takeaway with two cellophane-wrapped fortune cookies—might as well have a choice of futures. The last fortune he'd unfurled from one of these cookies had read: *Everything you try to endeavor will be successful.* Which he'd translated as everything you *try to try* . . . . He'd kept that one, thinking he couldn't do better in either promise or redundancy.

Bood met him at the door with high jumps—Ben holding the bag and its Styrofoam container up and away so Bood wouldn't catch the scent of food. He set the bag on the kitchen counter and scooped some kibbles into Bood's bowl, smacking his lips for the dog's benefit.

While Bood ate, Ben got his mailbox key and crossed his lawn to his mailbox, a brick affair with an anti-theft, drop-through mail compartment. He unlocked the engraved steel door at the lower half of the box and extracted the mail. Atop the pile of letters, ads, bills, and magazines lay a folded note sheet. Familiar by now. He unfolded it and read: *Someone could get hurt.*

Carrying his mail, he crossed back over his front lawn, into the house, and straight to the phone.

"How many of these personal notes you got?" Saenz asked.

"Three."

"Why didn't you tell me?"

"I'm telling you now. I gave the other notes to Forensics."

"Give them this one, too. Tell them I want it treated as a serious threat."

"The others were innocuous—you're clueless, you're running out of luck. Besides—"

"What do you think, Gallagher? Killer's after you?"

"Besides I don't even think they're from the killer."

"Who then? Why?"

"I don't know. Some nut case."

"Some nut case who knows where you live. And who just happens to know—"

"Know what? It's easy to find out where I live. And those notes haven't said anything that suggests special knowledge. Other than I'm leading the case."

"Same question. Why?"

"To fuck with my mind?"

"Why?"

Ben didn't have the answer.

He got the news on the kitchen TV and ate standing at the counter—mixing the orange chicken into the rice, peeling the shrimp and dousing them with red sauce and lemon juice, tossing the shells into the sink. Bood bumped his leg with his nose, and Ben held out a shrimp. The dog smelled it delicately and drew back with a look of such outrage that Ben laughed.

He rinsed down his food with cab and the sink with water, ran the disposal a few seconds, stuffed the spent lemon wedges into the unit and ran it again to neutralize the fishy smell. Then he swiped the dark granite of his countertop, washed his hands with a dollop of the smell-good stuff in the soap dispenser, rinsed and dried them, sniffed at his fingertips, and wrinkled his nose. He should have rubbed his fingers with those lemon wedges before pulverizing them in the disposal.

He tore open the cellophane on one of the fortune cookies, broke the cookie, extracted the fortune, and read: "Confucius say you have heart big as Texas."

Confucius knew about Texas?

The second cookie: "You will gain admiration from your pears."

Two keepers.

He poured the last of the cab into his glass, and he and Bood went upstairs to sprawl on one of the leather sofas in the media room. He hit the giant screen's remote, surfed a few channels and landed on a Bogie festival. He recognized the film on the screen, and he followed it for a bit, thinking the Cyberman case was equally convoluted, but at least no one had dragged him into an alley and kicked the shit out of him—as they were at this moment doing to Bogie.

Not yet, anyway . . . .

\#

The phone jerked him awake and into confusion. That it was Proudhorse was clear, but Philip and Vivian of "The Big Sleep" had disappeared. Instead, Ben found himself blinking at "To Have and Have Not"—at a world-weary Steve working for the French resistance, and blonde pickpocket Slim.

Proudhorse was apologizing. "I'm still at the office. Sorry it's so late."

Ben muted the TV.

"That's fine. Let's have it."

"Gaylord Longstreet Daniel. Born in Indianapolis October 24, 1958. Followed in his father's and grandfather's footsteps—they were also Episcopal priests. Dr. Daniel had two churches before All Saints. Ohio and Idaho. Small town called Lima, in Ohio. Went to the church there right out of divinity school, left when he was 31."

Proudhorse anticipated Ben's question.

"For a better offer. But he'd had some scrapes at the church. He was involved with at least three parishioners—sexual shenanigans, as one of the board members put it. But it sounded like more than shenanigans to me. A woman by the name of—"

Ben could hear Proudhorse breathing as he leafed through his notebook.

"Ruthanne Reed," Proudhorse continued. "Church organist. The scuttlebutt was she became distraught when Father Daniel dumped her. Anyway, she killed herself."

"Married?"

"Her husband began divorce proceedings when the affair came to light."

"Any suspicions about the suicide?"

"Doors were locked from the inside, and she left a note for her daughter. Ruthann's husband, Les Reed, said their daughter had discovered Mrs. Reed hoarding pills, and that they'd feared something like this."

"You spoke to the husband?"

"Yes. He was attending an out-of-town meeting the weekend Gaylord Daniel was killed. The meeting wrapped up Monday. Haven't verified that yet, but it'll be easy to check."

"What happened then? Was Daniel asked to leave?"

"You'd think so. But no. Guess he still had his elusive thing—charisma."

Ben's gaze had been following but not registering the flickering black-and-white images on the screen. But now he noticed Bacall and Bogie in what looked like a hotel room, their lips moving soundlessly but eyes saying plenty.

"Hang on a sec, Joe." He grabbed the remote. "I need to turn off the TV."

The huge screen went dark.

"Bacall was about to teach Bogie how to whistle."

Proudhorse chuckled.

"So Ohio wanted Daniel to stay?" Ben asked.

"Small community, word getting around, congregation building. They were sorry to see him leave. Hang on."

Ben heard paper rustling.

"Boise. The Idaho church. They're the ones asked him to leave. After only three years. Daniel still had his charisma. But he also had a noisy detractor—the mother of a fourteen-year-old boy."

"Don't tell me."

"Father Daniel denied it. The boy denied it. And the rumors were that the boy's mother was just another abandoned and vindictive lover. But it was all too much for Boise. They asked him to leave."

"Then All Saints?"

"Then All Saints. His experience in the other churches seems to have taught him discretion if not restraint. Rumors about liaisons with the ladies during his fifteen years here—including Verlie Mae Cheek—but no big blowups."

"She acknowledged an affair with Daniel?"

"Not really . . . Pratt asked her straight out, and Verlie Mae looked like she didn't know whether to be proud or ashamed. She—"

Ben yawned. "Let's hold the rest for tomorrow, Joe. I've got the big picture. No use making you repeat everything. Go home. Get some rest."

It was only after Ben was in bed—tossing from side to side and trying to accommodate the ache in his back and leg—that he considered Proudhorse's effort. Taking on whatever Ben asked.

A world of difference between Joe Proudhorse and Jack Malone.

CHAPTER TWENTY-TWO

Early Friday morning, August 24

Next morning everyone was in place—as if they'd left only to change clothes. The conference room was in pre-meeting confusion. Proudhorse and Hilda studied the contents of the folders in front of them. Pratt and Naldo jabbered about the gully-washing thunderstorm overnight and the rain still rattling the windows.

Malone, his face mangled with sleep and emanating both foul mood and nicotine funk, was at the table, his shirt and hair still wet from his run through the parking lot. He took up one whole end of the conference table, coffee cup in hand and the Arlington edition of the *Fort Worth Star-Telegram* laid out in front of him.

"Hey, hey," Ben said and plopped down a box of Krispy Kremes. He felt good. The pain had left his backside during the night, and he'd slept dreamlessly, having had a head start on the leather sofa upstairs. He'd awakened early to a crash of thunder and made the ten-minute drive to the office during a slackening of rain, the three tenors competing with the storm admirably on the car's CD player.

Hilda's eyes widened. "*You* bought Krispy Kremes?"

"Nope. Kenechi."

Hilda opened the box and admired its contents. "Cripes, maybe it's true about cops and doughnuts." She daintily lifted a pastry, and—sighing happily—consumed half in one bite.

"That's why they call us PIGs," said Pratt.

"Always hungry," Hilda said.

"Nah. PIG stands for plain, iced, or glazed."

Hilda laughed with her mouth full.

Ben cleared his throat and gave Proudhorse the nod.

Proudhorse stacked his notes in front of him and looked around the table with resignation. He didn't like giving presentations—mostly, Ben reflected, because he wasn't confortable with being the center of attention. But he gave them when he must, and they were accomplished with gravity and purpose. Although his voice was thin and his vocabulary simple, the deliberateness of his progress from one word to the next, one sentence to the next, one subject to the next, developed a compelling, convincing cadence.

"The Reverend Doctor Gaylord Longstreet Daniel," Proudhorse began. He proceeded with Daniel's vital stats, his career behind the pulpit, life behind the scenes—his account moving alongside an accompanying rumble of thunder and dying away on the word *charisma*.

The detectives were silent, and for an odd moment Ben thought they might applaud.

Hilda beamed at her partner.

"Let's move on to Verlie Mae Cheek," Ben suggested.

"Who the hell is Verlie Mae Cheek?" Malone said.

"Parishioner," Pratt said. "Nasty woman. Proudhorse and I—"

Proudhorse raised a hand. "Just a minute."

He opened a second folder and cleared his throat.

"Verlie Mae Cheek," he began, "looks like a hamster."

The room erupted into laughter.

"Bright little eyes, twitching nose," Proudhorse elaborated. "But a rodent just the same. And not quite as cute as a hamster. Wouldn't you say, Pratt?"

Pratt nodded. "Like I said. Nasty."

"In what way?" Ben asked.

"Constant snide innuendo."

"Concerning?"

"Concerning whoever. Other people in the parish."

"Especially women Father Daniel seemed to favor," said Proudhorse.

"But she went for Proudhorse," Pratt said, waggling his heavy salt-and-pepper brows. "Wowser, this gal. Sixtyish. Dye job. Kabuki makeup. Keeps touching Proudhorse's arm, like this." He gave Hilda's forearm a warm caress. "Tells him she's also part Navajo—"

Hilda's eyes were merry. "What'd Proudhorse say?"

Pratt grinned. "He said he was Comanche."

More laughter around the table, but Proudhorse looked up from his notes without amusement.

"She's interesting."

Hilda groaned. "Oh, man—"

"How so?" Ben asked.

"She said interesting things. And she keeps working her religion into the conversation—what she's done for the church, what she does for Jesus—she actually used those words. And all the time you're thinking what she does best is hate."

Everyone was paying attention.

"Go on," Ben said.

"She said she left for home right after the church supper Sunday night. But her next-door neighbor told me the light she leaves burning in her front window when she's gone was still on and the rest of the house dark when he went to bed. He had to take his dog out so he noticed."

Ben caught Hilda's surprise: her partner in the field alone?

136

"Time?" Ben asked.

"A little before eleven. He'd watched the ten o'clock news."

Ben thought a minute, doodling some circles onto a page of his notebook and turning them into bulls-eyes.

"OK, you think Verlie Mae Cheek's a bad piece of work. Bad enough to stand in a cemetery and shoot two people at close range? Bludgeon a sleeping man with an ax? Strangle a toddler?"

Proudhorse reflected. "One of the interesting things she said was if you want to hurt the parent, hurt the child."

Ben looked up from his notebook. "What was the context for that remark?"

"Sort of out of nowhere."

Pratt said, "She was talking about parenthood then, I think. She talked a blue streak, hard to keep up. She hated Claire Craven, that's clear."

"She said Claire Craven didn't want a baby and took something to cause a miscarriage," Proudhorse added, "and either that caused her baby's birth defects, or it was God's punishment. She said Claire Craven compounded her sin by sleeping with the doctor who fixed her son's cleft palate."

Rain slapped the windows in sheets.

"We asked her if Duff Craven had heard anything about all that," Pratt said. "And she said the Navajo had a saying—you can't wake a person who is pretending to be asleep."

Kenechi turned abruptly from the window and sought Ben's eye, his face urgent, but shaking his head a little when their eyes met. Ben gave him a half-nod and turned his attention back to Proudhorse.

"You want a little more time on this, Joe?" Ben asked Proudhorse.

"I'd like to see if I can find a connect between Verlie Cheek and J.J. or Toby." He rounded up his papers and closed the folders. "There's another Navajo saying."

Ben looked at him expectantly.

"There's nothing," Proudhorse said, "as eloquent as a rattlesnake's tail."

"The notes," Kenechi said abruptly from the window.

Proudhorse nodded. "I think she's the kind of person who'd warn before she struck. And not out of a sense of fair play, either."

"To get full satisfaction," Pratt said, looking at Proudhorse thoughtfully.

"OK," Ben said. "See what you come up with. You and Hilda."

It was as if a tide had shifted in the room. Ben put down his pen, and everyone rose in silence, gathering folders and notebooks and coffee cups.

"Hang on a second, Joe," Ben said. "The Ohio links—"

Ben noticed that Kenechi was lingering near the doorway and remembered his urgent face during the meeting—as though something had struck him. He signaled him to wait.

"The Ohio links—" he said to Proudhorse. "The woman who killed herself and her husband. When you've verified his alibi, look into the rest of the woman's family. See if anyone blames Daniel. Let's be sure we're not leaving any loose ends."

Proudhorse nodded.

"And, Joe. Don't carry on your own investigation. If you did. You know what I mean. Don't go into the field alone, without backup. Take Hilda. It's too risky, any number of ways."

"I know. I thought, though, with just the neighbors—"

"Not even then."

Proudhorse stiffened a little and turned away, reminding Ben how suited he was to his surname.

"Your report," Ben said. "Your work on All Saints. It's brilliant, all of it."

CHAPTER TWENTY-THREE

Midmorning Friday, August 24

"You had something on your mind during the meeting," Ben said to Kenechi.

"The Craven baby had surgery to correct his cleft palate. Verlie Cheek said Claire Craven slept with the surgeon."

"Yes."

"Who was that surgeon?"

It took Ben a second to realize the implications of Kenechi's query.

"Good question." He paused. "*Very* good question. You gonna get the answer?"

"I have the answer."

Hilda came down the corridor.

"I still like Duff Craven for it, boss."

"Duff Craven has an alibi."

She snorted. "Provided by his son."

"Five members of the congregation saw him leave," Ben said.

"Doesn't mean he didn't come back."

"No. But a couple of neighbors who were walking their dog saw Duff's pickup pull into his drive about the right time. Craven's house lights were on, and the pickup still in the drive when the couple walked back."

"Coulda been his son. I mean, two people live in that house."

"True."

"Or Duff could've come home, left again, walked to All Saints. It's only, what, a mile and a half?"

140

"So Ricky's home asleep while his dad's out killing his mother? Duff walks to All Saints and home again—this time in bloody clothes—and no one sees him either time?"

Hilda suppressed a smile. "Too Byzantine?"

"Hell, no. Nothing's too Byzantine. As we well know. What is it, Hilda? A feeling in your bones?"

Ben wasn't scoffing. He'd had that feeling plenty, and he respected it.

"What do I know about bones?" she said. "I'm just a worker bee."

Kenechi was fidgeting.

"Talk to his neighbors again," Ben told her.

"Why are you so set on Craven, Hilda?" Kenechi asked.

She looked shamefaced.

"Because he's an asshole."

She turned to leave, but Kenechi stopped her.

"Hang on a minute. I was just going to tell Ben who Ricky Craven's plastic surgeon was twenty-two years ago— the man Claire Craven slept with."

Ben was motionless, his blue eyes never leaving Kenechi's face. He studied Kenechi another millisecond, then turned to Hilda, who was nodding slowly, understanding everything.

"Break Craven's alibi if you can, Hilda."

When she was down the hall, Ben said: "I'd sure like a look at Craven's computer, Kenechi. We'd need a compelling reason. I mean something more compelling than a guy's an asshole. Nobody—certainly not Rolando Saenz—is going to let us go fishing"

"And we don't have that compelling reason, Ben. Everything comes back to ties."

Kenechi pulled out his notebook.

"Starting with J.J., we have ties between the Rubens and Jiggy. And from Jiggy to LeRoy Shatto to Lonnie Lacefield. From bookies Shatto and Lacefield to Toby, the gambler . . . tenuous, yes, but—"

"And how do we get from J.J. and Toby to the All Saints contingent, so to speak? Through this new link between Claire and Hayward Lugo? Otherwise, no shared activities, interests. Neither the Rubens nor the Lugos have religious connections in general—"

"To say the least."

"—let alone to All Saints in particular. Pratt and Naldo have chased down every avenue, every possibility. And come up dry."

"Malone could be right. Maybe there are no links."

"You believe that, Ken? You think this is random?"

"No."

"Anyway, now we have a connection between Hayward Lugo and the Cravens, even if twenty-two years old."

He produced a frustrated growl.

"What are we missing, Ken?"

Kenechi pressed his palm against the shallow bridge of his broad nose.

"You OK?" Ben asked.

He took his hand away. "I'm fine."

Ben was beginning to understand that Kenechi wasn't going to say anything to him about his finances or the uncertainty of his future with the force until he had to. He understood that Kenechi was worried about telling the chief but not his immediate superior. He also understood that he was dealing with the private problems of a private person, and that Kenechi had told the chief not only because he was chief but also because he trusted him. That kind of trust was worth something, and you either had it or you didn't.

He rose and pulled his door closed, crossed to the little round table at the other end of his office, pulled out one of the two chairs at the table, and sat. He shoved the other chair out with his foot and nodded toward it.

Kenechi traded chairs, crossed his legs, and looked at Ben with both curiosity and expectation.

"You asked before," Ben said, "about Andrew. About his being in prison. I cut you off."

The phone on Ben's desk buzzed, and he made the mistake of answering it.

"Sorry," he said when he put down the phone. "My car's in the shop—it's ready."

"If it's somewhere close, I can drop you. Grace has a doctor's appointment, and I'm meeting her there."

Ben found himself waiting, thinking here was another chance for Kenechi to mention Grace's pregnancy and the upheaval in his personal life.

"We were discussing Dayton Slaughter," Kenechi said.

Ben was lost.

"When we spoke about Andrew," he added.

"Oh. Dayton. Close friend. Surrogate father, really. He's godparent to both me and Andrew. Or, as he says: Always a godfather, never a god!"

Kenechi put his head back and let loose a short burst of soprano laughter. He didn't laugh often, and Ben loved to hear it.

"My father was killed in Vietnam," Ben said. "Before I was born. But Andrew's?" He shrugged. "Who knows."

He read Kenechi's puzzled silence. "Andrew's my half brother. We don't know who his dad is. By 'we,' I mean

Andrew and I." He smiled. "I'm guessing Ma knows. She's a non-talker."

He felt like adding: *Lot of that going around.*

"My father also was killed in war," Kenechi said.

"Biafra?"

"Also the rest of my family. I understand not wanting to talk about something."

Ben, who had been on the verge of asking Kenechi about the scar on his cheek, was glad he hadn't.

"The way I heard it, your brother got a raw deal," Kenechi said.

"Depends. A man died. It was the end of Andrew's junior year at Texas A&M. Another year of all-A's, headed for summa cum laude. He and some buddies were celebrating. Got drunk, thought they'd take a car idling outside a convenience store for a joyride. The car's owner ran from the store and grabbed the door handle."

Kenechi shook his head.

"He fell and went under. Died the next day. Browne Wilkins, his name was. Had a family, grandchildren. Andrew and his buddies were all charged with manslaughter."

Talking about it, Ben felt the same sick sense of waste he'd felt ten years ago—a decade that seemed like both yesterday and a lifetime. The year it took for the trial to roll around. Nell a basket case. Ben in Brazos County more than he was at Southern Methodist University working on his doctorate. Dayton down from Michigan every other weekend.

Fifteen years. With time off, ten.

"Seems harsh," Kenechi said. "Was he ever in trouble before?"

"Andrew? Hell no."

"His lawyer screw up?"

Ben flashed on Deacon Boggs—wild white hair, vested suit, cowboy boots, ice-blue eyes shadowed by the brim of his Stetson.

"Deke Boggs."

"The best," Kenechi said. "I don't get it."

But Deke Boggs had got it, Ben thought. Right-wing bible-thumpers, he'd said, meanest dang people in the world.

"Bottom line, a man died."

"There can be extenuating circumstances even when someone dies. Things aren't always black and white."

"The law is."

Kenechi studied him. Ben's phone buzzed again, but he ignored it.

"What are his chances for parole?" Kenechi asked.

"Coming up. The closer it gets, the less sure we are that we can do even another week, let alone six months. For ten years, we've worried that he's going to get hurt in there. I mean really hurt. His nose has been broken twice, eyes blacked. But I know that only because I saw it. I wonder what we don't see. So does Ma."

It was a long speech for Ben, and Kenechi took his time digesting it. Over his shoulder, Ben saw Sly signaling him through his window, saw him mouth something he didn't understand. He acknowledged Sly with a gesture, which Kenechi caught and rose.

"He can *only* get hurt in there," he said. Ben had noticed many times that when Kenechi spoke softly, his voice went deep and cottony, as if he'd swallowed a mouthful of fog.

The opposite happened when he laughed—his voice moved up the scale an octave.

He can only get hurt in there. A blunt and sweeping response, but delivered gently, and Ben appreciated its honesty. Tacit in Kenechi's words was an understanding he and Nell never voiced. A broken nose heals. What of the hurts that don't heal?

CHAPTER TWENTY-FOUR

Late morning Friday, August 24

"Jiggy Ruben's here," Sly said. "Room two."

"Get everyone together, Sly," Ben said. "Kenechi can back up. I want Hilda and Proudhorse in the room, too. The others can observe."

Room two was a fusty little windowless space with bare walls and functional furniture—a central table outfitted with two comfortable leather chairs and an uncomfortable wooden one for the interviewee. Audio and video equipment recorded whatever happened or was said in that room, and a large mirror on one wall masked an observation window.

Jeremiah Ruben stood with his back to them—already interesting, Ben thought, because most people waiting in that room faced the mirror, the only visual relief on those unadorned gray-green walls.

Jiggy was a neckless chunk of a man, his overbuilt muscles struggling beneath a layer of lard. He leaned back on his heels a little, probably to balance his gut. From the back, his jug ears stuck out like handles from the carrot-colored fringe of his tonsured head.

"Pillsbury Doughboy on steroids," Hilda whispered.

"Check out that shirt," said Naldo. The tropical print of purple and pink made Jiggy's back and shoulders look immense. "Must take a tent to cover those shoulders."

"Wardrobe by Barnum and Bailey," Proudhorse said.

Hilda stifled a guffaw.

"Why do you whisper in here?" Proudhorse asked her, turning up his own volume a little. "He can't hear you."

Jiggy, as if hearing, turned and seemed to look straight at them. Hilda drew back from the glass.

Without looking away from the mirror, Jiggy crossed to the table and took the single wooden chair stationed there, the uncomfortable hard chair with the sloping seat that no one could sit in without slipping forward. He turned the chair a little to the side so he could face the mirror and sat all the way back, resting his gut on his thighs, and peered into the mirror.

"Geez, let's go in," Hilda breathed.

Jiggy's gaze made Ben uneasy, too. But he took a second to study him further. Jiggy was approaching fifty and looked every bit of it. He had a wizened quality, despite his heft. Sparse brows and orange stubble. A simian ridge low on his forehead. And amid that ugliness an aristocratic, aquiline nose and wide, handsome lips. Or wide amphibian lips, depending.

"Jeremiah was a bullfrog," Hilda murmured.

Ben squinted at the tattoos covering both Jiggy's forearms but couldn't tell what they were.

Jiggy looked at them briefly and without interest when they entered the room. He shuttered his eyes behind heavy, lashless lids and worked on a hangnail. Ben took a swivel chair at one end of the table, and Kenechi took the other. Hilda and Proudhorse leaned against the wall.

"Jeremiah Ruben," Ben said. "I'm Ben Gallagher. This is —"

"Call me Jiggy."

Ben saw that the mélange of tattoos snaking over his forearms were roses—blossoms and buds that seemed to writhe on a field of dark blue. He spoke the preamble for the tape recorder and got right to the point.

"Where were you Sunday night, Jiggy?"

"And hello to you, too. I'm here of my own volition, and I'm assuming I can leave the same way." Jiggy's voice was a thin treble that belied his brawn, and his expression showed nothing—not surprise, not wariness, not curiosity. "My lawyer doesn't know I'm here. Do I need to call him?"

"Depends upon what you have to hide. Sunday night?"

"Poker?"

"From when to when?"

"Nine, thereabouts. One, two in the morning."

Convenient game, Ben thought, convenient time span. "Where?"

"My place."

"The apartment on Green Oaks?"

"My office. Midlothian."

Ben raised a brow and waited. Jiggy did, too. Ben let loose a dramatic sigh, and Jiggy put up a hand, said *yeah, yeah,* and rolled his eyes—just a little, not enough to piss anyone off.

"We like playing there. Out of the way, quiet little group, nobody to bother us."

"You're talking about your office at the so-called stables, in Midlothian."

"Right."

"What you got going out there besides cards?"

"Guess I don't understand the question."

"Who else was there Sunday night?"

Jiggy gave his tattoo a scratch.

"What are the rose tats all about?" Ben asked.

Jiggy's sharp little eyes swung to Ben's. "That's what they're about. The Rose Tattoo."

"Tennessee Williams' play?"

Jiggy put on a smile that looked like a gas pain and surveyed the room.

"Blues, hard rock," Hilda said. "Australian band—bassist learned his guitar in prison."

"Had street cred," said Jiggy.

"Began like the late '70s." Hilda said. "Musta been your heyday."

Ben let all that sink in and returned to his line of questioning.

"Who else was playing poker Sunday night?"

"Half a dozen guys, maybe."

"We'll need their names."

Jiggy shook his head and started to speak, but Ben stopped him.

"We'll need their names."

"I was gonna say: We're on a first-name basis."

Ben waited, returning Jiggy's frog-like gaze beat for beat.

"Two of the guys I know from way back, though. Shatto and Lacefield."

Ben wrote and looked again at Jiggy, who scratched through his orange stubble experimentally, as if gauging its growth.

"You know what we need, goddammit," Ben said. "Give it up. Or don't give it up and prepare to stay a while."

"*LeRoy* Shatto and *Lonnie* Lacefield."

Ben flipped to an empty page in his notebook. "They know the other guys?"

"Maybe."

"Or maybe not. And maybe you don't know who was there because you weren't there."

Jiggy examined his ragged cuticles again.

"Besides Shatto and Lacefield, who can corroborate your story?"

"My story?"

"Your alibi."

Jiggy pulled a small rectangular case of clear plastic from the breast pocket of his Hawaiian shirt, thumbed the red cover, and shook a plastic toothpick into his palm.

"You know what?" He stuck the pick between two molars and worked it back and forth. "I've said all I'm going to."

"Not hardly, buddy."

"I can rephrase it. I don't know what's on your mind, but I've said all I'm going to without my lawyer sitting here beside me." He examined the end of the toothpick and stuck it back in his mouth. "Without my lawyer sitting here protecting my rights."

Ben saw that Jiggy's nails were bitten to the quick, an expanse of callused flesh at the tip of each stub-like finger. He had seen it before—an outward sign of the inner tension it creates to appear nerveless. He was about to decide that Jiggy Ruben's control was that sort of sham when the man abruptly yawned, neither covering his mouth nor excusing himself. Ben had seen plenty of interview room yawns. They were usually tension relievers, or a side effect of hyperventilation, or just bogus—a way to borrow time. But this was a real yawn—relaxed and spontaneous. Jiggy's jaw creaked a little at the top of the yawn, and his eyes watered as he exhaled.

Joe Proudhorse, arms crossed, shifted his weight against the wall with a look of such black intensity that Jiggy seemed to notice him for the first time.

"What's up with the wooden Indian?" he asked.

151

"Tell you what, buddy," Ben said. "You sit there and think about your rights. And I'll think about November 10, 1980. And about Amos and Abel Blum—and their rights."

Jiggy didn't move a muscle.

"Remember that night, Jiggy? The night you killed two old men and ransacked their apartment? Stole the jewelry from the shop downstairs?"

Ben reached into his pocket and took out an evidence bag, studied it just long enough for Jiggy Ruben to wonder what it was. He opened the bag, withdrew the watch he'd taken from Zack Ruben, and slid it across the table toward Jiggy.

"This watch was handmade by Amos Blum. You can see his mark if you know what you're looking for. It was stolen the night he was killed."

Ben gave it a little time to sink in before continuing.

"You stole it. And stupidly kept it. And years later gave it to your nephew as a graduation present. You thought you got away with murder, didn't you, Jiggy? All those years ago."

Jiggy sat stock still, hands folded over his girth, a roll of fat taut beneath his chin, not a twitch of cheek or brow. But something had changed. His no-color eyes, already veiled, seemed to slide out of focus as if behind a translucent membrane.

"November 10, 1980," Ben prompted, pushing his swivel chair back and coming around the corner of the table, closer to Jiggy. "Amos and Abel Blum."

"My lawyer is Jeremy Rivkin." Jiggy reached into the breast pocket of his Hawaiian shirt and laid his mobile on the table. "You wanna call him or should I?"

Ben closed the space between them in one stride and gathered a bunch of the tropical print shirtfront in one fist. Jiggy didn't flinch or show surprise. But surprise was palpable in the room, and Ben felt it—his colleagues wondering if he was losing it again. But he was as aware of his movements and intention as he was of the video cam whirring away silently on the wall.

Because now he knew. It wasn't just that feeling in his bones. The truth was in the defensive blockade that slid into place around Jiggy Ruben when he heard the name Blum—a defense decades in the making.

Ben moved to the mirror and looked into it without seeing himself, imagining Pratt and Naldo and Malone on the other side, looking back at him. He let his anger drain away, and deep in his brain, two tales unfolded side by side:

Twenty-year-old Jiggy Ruben beating and shooting and robbing two old men. Whatever else there was, that was a circumstance Ben knew.

And twenty-year-old Andrew Gallagher getting drunk and stupid over a Ford Crown Victoria, and driving over its owner. But Andrew went to prison, had been in prison for nearly ten years. While Jiggy played Texas Hold 'Em and stabled vintage cars . . . .

And that, too, was a circumstance Ben knew.

He went to the door, jerked it open, and stepped into the corridor—Kenechi, Hilda, and Proudhorse staying in place. Ben stepped to the observation room door and beckoned, and Naldo came forward, inquisitive.

"Find LeRoy Shatto and Lonnie Lacefield asap and bring them in," Ben said. "I'm guessing Jiggy Ruben will try to contact them as soon as he leaves here, but I don't want him to succeed. I'll delay him as long as I can, but I can't hold him. When he leaves, I want him to have a real clumsy tail, one he can't miss. I want him to know-"

"You want him to know he's being tailed," Naldo said.

Ben looked at him a long moment, and Naldo put his hands in front of his chest, defensively, palms out.

"Just making sure."

Jiggy was as Ben had left him, looking at nothing, chair a little sideways, an elbow resting on the table, the other arm laid on his belly.

"You'll be free to go in a few minutes, Jiggy," Ben said.

"Why in a few minutes? Why not now?"

Ben pulled his swivel chair around the corner of the conference table, parked it close to Jiggy, and sat so they were almost knee to knee. "But we'll see you again real soon. Don't plan anything special."

He let his gaze bore into Jiggy's and hoped his eyes said clearly: *Got you, Jeremiah Ruben. After all this time!*

#

In the corridor, Hilda said, "Rose Tattoo is also a computer adventure game. The Lost Files of the Sherlock Holmes series."

"A detective game. I remember. Red roses seem ubiquitous in this case."

"What do you think?" Kenechi said.

Ben chewed his lip, his eyes on Kenechi's.

"I can see Jiggy Ruben doing it all."

"Even J.J.? A child? A relative?"

Malone caught up with them.

"I can find out who else was at the Sunday night poker game," he said.

154

"Can you?" Ben asked.

"Yes."

Ben didn't ask him how.

CHAPTER TWENTY-FIVE

Friday midday, August 24

Ben turned south on Cooper and cruised to Cain Place. Approaching 112, he was struck again by the contrast between house and grounds—the drab bungalow and the well-tended lawn and flowerbeds.

He found Duff Craven inside with a man Craven introduced as John Cheek. As in Verlie Mae Cheek, Ben guessed.

"John's about to leave," Craven said. "We're discussing root rot on woody ornamentals."

"Mr. Cheek," Ben said. He showed his badge. "I need a few minutes with you, too, before you leave."

Cheek scowled.

"Now's fine."

Craven moved away, and Ben began without preamble.

"You and Claire Craven were overheard quarreling at All Saints. I want to know what that quarrel was about."

"I don't see how that's your business."

"I'm investigating Claire Craven's murder. It's my business."

"Fine. I'll tell you what that quarrel was about." He paused. "It was about that bitch's wagging tongue."

Ben saw that Cheek was so tight-lipped that the tiny lines radiating from his mouth were little white spokes.

That bitch's wagging tongue.

Not wagging anymore, Ben thought.

"Tell me about the quarrel."

"She spread it around that I have a habit. That I'm squandering my wife's money on gambling."

"Are you?"

"You ever play a friendly game of poker, detective?" Cheek moved to the door. "Am I arrested, or am I leaving?"

Craven followed Cheek out the door, and Ben studied the Cravens' living room. He saw no effort to decorate—no pictures on the walls, no objects on tabletops, the mismatched lamps merely functional. Seating was a taupe sectional, overlarge for the room, and an overstuffed armchair striped in earth tones.

A short corridor off the living room showed four doors, two of them open. Ben glanced through the window at Craven and Cheek talking in the drive and stepped toward the first open door. It was a stuffy little bathroom, its single small window facing the north and affording little light. The next door was the Cravens' bedroom, oppressive with dark walls and drawn shades. Ben saw a hastily made bed, its sole covering a wrinkled top sheet. Against one wall stood an old-fashioned dresser, a mixture of drawers and shelves, the latter displaying framed photos of various vintage. A computer stood on a small desk angled in the corner, its screen dark. Ben stepped quickly to the keyboard and tapped a key.

Nothing happened.

He again ducked his head into the hall to peer through the front window—Duff Craven discussing root rot on woody ornamentals. Back in the bedroom, Ben studied the pictures on the dresser. A wood-framed photo showed a younger Duff, his carefully groomed hair and brows still dark. A more recent shot had Duff sitting in the striped armchair in the living room, his knobbed hands flat on his thighs and shaggy brows hiding colorless and impassive eyes. Front and center was a gold-framed shot of a smiling, younger Claire, a pointed foil hat on her cloud of dark hair, a drink in one hand and a cigarette in the other.

There were no pictures of the Cravens together, or of their infant, but a studio portrait memorialized the toddler—holding a red ball, withered leg out of view, cleft palate repaired but still obvious in the retouched photo.

Loose pictures rested on a shelf and, off to the side, a single old snapshot with deckle edges lay face down beneath a satin-smooth seashell. Ben set the shell aside and picked up the photo. It was a slightly out-of-focus image of a young, slender Gaylord Longstreet Daniel leaning against an iron rail with nothing but the shining sea behind him—hatless, grinning, sun full on his face and wind in his hair, legs crossed at the ankles, at ease against the rail. The just-grown Man of God, thought Ben.

He shuffled through the loose snapshots. Claire posing on the arm of the striped chair, now occupied by a substantial and middle-aged Dr. Daniel—Claire leaning toward him but not touching, her right knee hiked to sit sidesaddle on the overstuffed chair arm, tight skirt hiked a little, too, showing her shapely legs, her feet encased in the T-strapped shoes she'd worn in death.

Several dog-eared business cards, held together with a paper clip, also lay on a shelf. Ben removed the clip and glanced through them. The Reverend Daniel's familiar card. One from Shear Class hairstyles. Another from Sole Purpose, which seemed either a shoestore or a shoe repair.

Another from Zack's Fitness.

Ben's breath quickened. A link from Claire to Ruben!

Ben turned to what was obviously Claire's side of the bed. On a nightstand shelf tumbled a messy stack of paperback romances. A fuchsia dressing gown and matching negligee lay tossed on a velvet bench tucked under a vanity. Cosmetics were spread over the vanity's surface along with brushes and combs, bottles of designer perfume, an open jar of cleansing cream . . . .

"What is it you're looking for in here, exactly?" Duff Craven said from the doorway.

"Did Claire belong to Zack's Fitness? Or go there?"

"Do you have a warrant for this search?"

"Zack's Fitness?"

"Never heard of it. Never heard of him."

"His card's in your bedroom."

Craven bent stiffly to pull open the four short drawers of Claire's dresser. They were a tumble of filmy lingerie and nightwear. "Your people already pretty much tossed this place. But if you want another look, have at it."

Ben was acutely aware that his solitary visit was not protocol. Nevertheless, he felt beneath the dresser drawers and around their sides and bottoms. From one, he took a purple satin ribbon, creased at four points, its ends tied in a small bow—the kind of ribbon that might have bound a packet of letters. From another, he withdrew an envelope, its flap tucked inside. Ben pulled out the flap and ran his thumb over the bills inside the envelope. Even a cursory glance revealed ten or twelve hundreds, a few fifties, a handful of twenties and tens.

He looked at Duff Craven.

"Mad money," Craven said, his face registering nothing.

"That's a lot of mad."

Craven abruptly left the room, the door swinging closed behind him.

Ben cast a last look around the room and headed for the door. But he sensed rather than heard someone on the other side. He snatched it open, expecting to find Duff Craven lurking there. Instead, he found a thin, heavily made-up woman with owlish eyes, a beak of a nose, black hair pulled tightly into a bun at the back of her head. She was cradling a tissue-wrapped bundle of red roses as if strutting down a pageant runway.

She gasped. "What are you doing in there?"

"What are you doing out here?"

Her restless eyes roamed the room behind him, lighting like a fly on this object and that, and at last returned to his face. Ben remembered Pratt's description: Bright little eyes, twitching nose but not as cute as a hamster.

"Who are you," she demanded.

"I'm the police. And you're Verlie Mae Cheek."

"What?" She drew back. "How do you know that?"

"As I said, I'm the police."

"Why would the police know me? I only ever spoke with two detectives, and you're not one of them."

"What are you doing here, Verlie Mae?"

"Well, really—" Seeing Ben's expression, she broke off. "I'm here with my husband. We're friends."

"You and your husband?"

She snorted. "Friends of Duff."

"Ah."

"*Ah?* Ah! What do you mean by that?"

Ben pushed past her and her roses, their thorns catching at his sleeve.

"Well, really," she said again.

160

He headed outside, where Craven was tending his roses.
Ben held out the empty ribbon.

"What did this ribbon hold, Mr. Craven? Love letters?
Correspondence between Claire and Gaylord Daniel?"

"What brought you here, detective? You must have had a
reason."

Ben kept his eyes on the older man. "I understand
Hayward Lugo was your son's surgeon."

For once, Duff Craven showed his emotion, an amalgam
of surprise and rage.

"Why would that interest you?" he asked.

"We're interested in anyone connected to Claire in
certain ways."

"That was more than twenty years ago. And Hayward
Lugo has no connection to Claire, certain or otherwise."

"Still."

Duff stooped and grabbed a length of sturdy rosebush
cane lying on the grass, toothed with needle-sharp thorns.
He hurled it toward Ben, who ducked as the jagged cane
sailed over his head. Immediately there was a small shriek
behind him. Verlie Mae stood with her hand to her face,
John Cheek a little behind her. A long, bloody scratch
scored her forehead, and the thorny cane dangled from her
dark hair.

CHAPTER TWENTY-SIX

Friday afternoon, August 24

Ben and his team traipsed to room two for the second time that day, entered the observation room, and peered through the one-way window.

LeRoy Shatto was out of the straight-back chair and ambling the room's perimeter—a rangy man, tall and broad but lean, as flat front and back as an ironing board. Origin unknown, Ben thought: golden skin, hyperthyroid eyes with pupils the color of Sultana raisins, a touch of rust to his nappy locks.

He reminded Ben of a wooden puppet Dayton had given him when he was a boy. It had jointed hips and knees and was suspended above a plywood paddle. Tap the paddle, and it bounced against the puppet's feet and made it dance. Its loose-jointed legs buckled and flapped, knees bent and straightened, feet tapped heel and toe.

It was in that manner that Shatto slapped loose-jointed around the room, softly whistling "Bobby McGee."

"Bo Jangles," whispered Hilda. She stood on tiptoe. "What's he doing?"

"Dancing. Whistling," Ben said. "Singing now."

"Singing?"

"Feelin' near as faded as his jeans."

Hilda listened. "He's coming to the hard part."

"The lah-dee-dahs," Naldo said.

Shatto pivoted rhythmically at the corners of the interview table, thrusting his big head forward with each step, preparing to tap, shuffle, and turn. But Ben and

Kenechi entered the room, followed by Hilda and Proudhorse, and he stopped roaming and slid smoothly onto the straight-backed chair.

"How ya doing, LeRoy?" Ben asked, taking a seat at the table.

"Aw, you know. Same ol' same ol'. Am I arrested?"

"I don't know. What have you done?"

Shatto looked innocent.

"I brought you in to answer some questions."

"Huh. Well, on most things, I don't got a clue. Just so's you know."

Ben spoke quietly, giving Shatto time between questions. The silences were filled with the sound of a wobbly ceiling fan churlishly stirring up some modestly cooled air.

Shatto had a hard time sitting still, his butt sliding on the slope of the oak seat, feet shifting, sharp knees roving from side to side beneath his roomy trousers.

But he had a harder time answering. Cracked his large knuckles. Scratched his large head. Checked out the room's bare walls and the no-color tweed carpeting beneath his Fred Astaire spectator shoes.

Ben kept the questions coming: Zack and Lulu Ruben? J.J.? Drugs? Steroids? Zack's Fitness?

LeRoy pondered each question.

Hmm. Clueless. I told you. Was I ever there? Ain't never been there, neither. Can't say I know about that. Can't say I know about that neither.

Ben said, "Seems you don't know much, LeRoy."

"I know *that's* true."

"Where were you Sunday night?"

Sunday night? Last Sunday night? Poker game. Who? Hmm! Not sure I caught their names. Lonnie was there. Yeah, Lonnie Lacefield. Jiggy Ruben? Hmm, was that the night—was he there? Maybe not. Coupla guys in and out the game. Don't know, exactly.

"*Exactly* is what we need here," Ben said.

Shatto chewed his lips and moved his big amber eyes from Ben to Kenechi and back.

"Yeah," he said so softly he could have been speaking to himself. "What you need. And what I need." Turning on his chair, Shatto scrutinized the other detectives in the room, then the two-way mirror on the wall.

"The man. He behind the mirror? Be lookin' at me right now?"

With a start, Ben thought of Malone hanging back, not following Ben into the interview room but taking up a position at the observation window. He looked at Kenechi, who looked back.

"Who do you mean by the man, Leroy?"

"I been clean, detective," Shatto said, appeal in his woolly voice.

"Was Jiggy Ruben with you Sunday night?"

Shatto searched the ceiling.

"Tell us," Ben urged. He rose, folder in hand, and walked behind Shatto, forcing him to turn on the oak seat, cranking his head up awkwardly.

"LeRoy. You know Toby Lugo?"

He shook his head.

"Gaylord Daniel."

No.

"Claire Craven. Duff Craven."

No. And no.

"Where were you on the night of November 10, 1980?"

The switch brought Shatto's prominent golden eyes to rest on Ben.

"*1980?*" he asked. "What you talkin', bro?"

"November 10, 1980, LeRoy. The night Amos and Abel Blum were murdered."

"Guess I don't know 'bout that neither."

"Blum Brothers Custom Jewelry."

Shatto looked away.

"This is hard, isn't it, LeRoy. Be so nice just to tell the truth, wouldn't it. Little shop in Dallas. West End. One of the Blums was a piano teacher." Ben paused. "*My* piano teacher, LeRoy. I found the bodies."

Now he understood. Ben saw it. This guy Gallagher was settling a score, and he wasn't going away.

"Aw, man, shit, another century. Why go there. How do I know where I was some night more'n twenty years ago?"

"We're going there, LeRoy. And we'll take along stuff we didn't have then."

Forensics. Ben could tell Shatto understood that, too.

"Like I said, I been clean, detective. Not squeaky, but clean. Huntsville. Been there, done that. Your worst nightmare, man. I ain't goin' back."

When Shatto mentioned Huntsville, Ben felt the other detectives' eyes on him.

"I *ain't* goin' back," Shatto said, just above a whisper.

"You were raised in Dallas."

"Lotsa people raised in Dallas didn't kill no Blum brothers."

"How old were you in '80, LeRoy? Fifteen? Sixteen? Jiggy Ruben the older guy you worked for? You and Lonnie Lacefield?"

Shatto was startled. "I don't know, man. You the one got the folder."

"Younger than Jiggy Ruben, anyway. Guess the three of you raised a little hell together, eh? But Jiggy the man, you and Lacefield being minors. Let's see—" He looked at the folder, pretended to read while Shatto shuffled his long feet and sighed.

Ben got up and walked off to the side. From this angle, he could see Shatto's large hands in his lap, trying unsuccessfully to keep still. And he could see in the reflection of the overhead lights on the bare tabletop a multitude of fingerprints from a multitude of clammy hands. He stepped to the water cooler outside the door, pulled a cone-shaped paper cup from the dispenser and filled it from the spigot. Handed it to Shatto, who looked at it suspiciously, then took it, drank it off, and proceeded to fold it into precise pleats.

"I see you lived a couple of blocks from the Blums' apartment," Ben said.

Shatto didn't look up. He was busy with the cup, pleating away.

"You said you were clean, LeRoy. Stay that way. Jiggy wasn't at the game Sunday night. Say it."

Shatto turned so his back was to the observation mirror.

"That what you want? Be a dangerous thing to say." It was just a whisper. "Best not to say things ain't true."

Ben sat again and looked at Kenechi, who turned down the corners of his mouth and shook his head. Ben laid Amos Blum's watch on the table in front of Shatto. Then he wrote his cell and home phone numbers on the back of his business card and laid it beside the watch.

"We don't need to talk about this right now," he said. "But another time, soon."

Shatto stared at the watch and the card.

"You can go, LeRoy," Ben said, the man meeting his eyes now. Ben didn't say: *You and I will talk again.* He knew Shatto knew that. And he also knew that it was OK. Ben didn't sense fear in LeRoy Shatto. He sensed something else—fatigue, resignation, relief, something like that.

Once, when Jack Malone's girls were small, Malone had car trouble, and Ben drove him to a dance studio on Park Row to pick up the girls. They got there early, and Ben went in to wait with Malone. The dance instructor was putting the little girls through their paces, and there were Malone's girls, right up in front in their pink leotards and shiny black Mary Janes, tapping away.

"Heel! Toe!" the instructor cried. "Back! Side! Front! Clap!"

That's what Ben remembered as Shatto unfolded himself from the chair, reached the doorway in one beat, spread his broad hand, and ducked away as if the door frame were a curtain.

HeelToe! BackSideFrontClap!

"Exit stage right," Hilda said.

Kenechi said, "What do you think, Ben?"

Ben rose stiffly. "I think I'd kill for his joints."

CHAPTER TWENTY-SEVEN

Friday night, August 24

Ben's phone rang a little after midnight.

"It's probably too late to call," said LeRoy Shatto's whispery voice.

Ben was instantly alert. "Of course it isn't."

"I just wanted to say, if you want to talk, we can do that."

Ben pulled to the edge of the bed and turned on the lamp.

"Where are you?"

"I don't mean now, man."

"Now's OK, LeRoy."

"Tomorrow's OK, too."

"Yes, tomorrow's OK, too."

"I wanted to call while I had my nerve. Since you so kindly gave me your numbers and all that."

Ben could see the man in his mind's eye, the rust-tinged nappy locks, the large amber eyes.

"Can I get a preview, LeRoy?"

"Jiggy Ruben was at the poker game Sunday night. The whole time."

"You've talked to Jiggy."

"No. But whether I talked to him or not, he was at the game. I know that's not what you want to hear, man."

"I want to hear the truth, LeRoy."

"You just did."

Ben was silent for a moment, Ben trying to figure it out.

Shatto said: "Those old men."

Ah.

"The Blums," Ben said.

"I didn't kill those old men. I never killed nobody."

"I believe you, LeRoy. This what you want to talk about."

"I guess," he said after a long silence.

Another silence. When he spoke again, his furry voice was even softer.

"I was only a kid. And I done some time when I grew up. I thought since I done some time . . . ."

"That you were square?"

"Something like that."

"Let's talk now. I could meet you. Or pick you up, bring you back here. No one would know."

"We can talk tomorrow." What little energy was left in Shatto's voice drained away, leaving it flat and fuzzy. "If I don't run."

"You gonna run, LeRoy?"

"No, man. I'll call."

"Try my cell or office number if I don't answer here."

Shatto hung up, and Ben sat on the edge of the bed, phone in hand. The Blum case. He could wait a little—he knew the important part now, and knew it the important way. In his bones.

So Jiggy was playing poker Sunday night. His link was to the Rubens anyway—not to Gaylord Daniel and Claire. But whoever killed J.J. and Toby killed Daniel and Claire, too. Right?

Right?

Ben believed Shatto. He knew he'd have given him the story he thought Ben wanted if he could. But he couldn't. LeRoy Shatto had lived a dark life. He was a thief and pusher and petty criminal and who knew what else. But he wasn't a liar. Ben had seen it before—scoundrels who managed to rationalize any number of misdeeds, but somehow clung to a scrap of personal innocence, a fragmented code of morality. What was it John Dillinger, Public Enemy No. 1, said when he was arrested?

I don't see how I could have done anything any different.

Jiggy had an alibi for Sunday night. That put a hitch in Ben's train of thought, which had been chugging away smoothly but was now rolling out of the station and out of sight.

And Ben standing on the platform, going nowhere.

OK, he told himself. Connect the dots, starting with the victims. The number of connections was growing, with Gaylord Daniel the odd man out.

Toby Lugo kept cropping up. But not a direct connection to Daniel and Claire. They'd focused on the gambling debt angle. Maybe they should talk to people Toby knew outside that angle. Cecilia Lugo had mentioned a girl. Hayward Lugo had discounted her as "just a friend." Maybe that's what they needed. And maybe she was more than just a friend.

Ben picked up his notebook from the nightstand, paged back till he found the name. Trudelle Williams.

He leafed through the notebook for a while but at last turned off the lamp and lay down again, Shatto's wooly voice echoing in his ears, his thoughts a jumble. At length, his mind slowed, and he felt himself go adrift . . . and the phone rang, jerking him back. His digital clock showed it was almost two. He grabbed the phone and checked the display but didn't recognize name or number.

"I'm the bartender at the Texas Toast," the voice said.

The Texas Toast. Ben knew of it vaguely. An unsavory place on East Division.

"This guy Malone," the bartender said. "Somebody you know? We're closing, and he's pretty far gone to dump on the street. Guess he's a cop, says he's your partner."

"Drunk?"

The caller laughed shortly. "Drunk is the least of this guy's problems."

Ben gritted his teeth and said he was on his way. Threw on a pair of chinos and a black pullover, slipped his bare feet into sandals, grabbed his watch and wallet and keys. It didn't take more than twenty minutes to get to the Texas Toast, especially with Arlington streets two-in-the-morning empty. And especially flaming mad and driving like it. But when Ben got there, Malone was out on the deserted sidewalk anyway, sitting on the curb, head down, his complexion sickly under the streetlight.

Ben shut off the ignition, got out of the Lexus, opened the passenger door and, without speaking, wrestled his partner into the car. It wasn't easy—Malone was the next thing to a dead weight. Under the dome light, Ben saw the remnants of vomit on Malone's turquoise golf shirt, and something else—a thin trickle of blood from his left nostril.

"Christ," Ben muttered.

Quickly, he thrust Malone's legs inside the Lexus and backed away—bumping into someone standing on the sidewalk behind him.

He wheeled and saw a tall, sallow-faced guy in baggy Bermuda shorts.

"I'm the bartender. Texas Toast," the guy said. "The one who called."

"Thanks."

Or not.

The bartender hitched up his shorts and stooped to peer at Malone, who was breathing noisily in Ben's passenger seat.

"Arlington's finest," he said.

Ben said nothing. That's all there was to say.

"So you'll know, if you don't already," the bartender said. "Your buddy's a user."

Duh.

"He busts people around here. Steals their stuff."

Ben inhaled, exhaled. "Thanks again."

"Somebody should do something," the bartender said.

No kidding.

The bartender stuck out a hand, and they shook. He had fingers like latex tentacles, limp and cool. Ben slammed Malone's door and crossed in front of the car, the motor ticking away its heat into the August night. He eased into the driver's seat, his back protesting, carefully pulled his own door closed, turned the key, and kicked the engine back to life.

He glanced at Malone and clenched his jaw so hard it hurt. Cracko Jacko. Dirty cop. His partner. He felt heat in his cheeks and was astonished at the depth of his anger.

Malone roused a little, said something indecipherable.

Futile to talk to him. But Ben couldn't help it.

"Your days are numbered, Jacko."

Malone surprised him by muttering, "You been a good partner, a good . . . ."

"I've been a good resource, Jack. That's all. A resource you've exhausted. Like everyone you come in contact with."

He tore away from the Texas Toast and through the streets, braking hard at the lights, careening around corners, lurching to a stop in front of Malone's dinky little frame house, its enclosed porch and postage-stamp yard dark under a canopy of large old oaks. He reached across Malone and flipped the door handle. The door swung open.

"Sleep it off, Jack."

Malone began the laborious project of getting out of the car and disappeared, the door open. Ben reached over with a grunt, twisting to pull the door closed. Pain streaked down his torso from neck to thigh. He straightened with difficulty. He knew Malone was on the ground and wished he had whatever it took to roar off and leave him there. But for all he knew, Malone's legs were beneath the car. With a curse, he flung open the door and slid out, his back wrenching, and found a befuddled Malone sitting on his butt on the grass. Ben went through his pockets, found his house key, and gave him a little push to straighten him up. Malone fell straight back, flat on the grass, his heels on the sidewalk.

Both the entrance light and the porch's interior lights were out, bathing the place in darkness. The light from the corner streetlamp was blocked by the tall oaks, their leafy branches casting moving shadows across the lawn. Ben moved up the three cracked steps into the black box of Malone's enclosed porch. Darker than he thought, too dark to manage key and lock. He'd get the flashlight from the car. He was turning back toward the narrow entryway when the policeman's scalp-prickling second sense told him he was not alone. At that instant, he felt someone else's presence, felt a movement to his right, began to turn—and his head exploded in a red fury.

And oblivion.

CHAPTER TWENTY-EIGHT

Saturday morning, August 25

Ben woke to unfamiliar sounds. Snatches of hushed conversation. Rapid footsteps approaching, diminishing. Rubber wheels. Doors opening, swinging closed. The small sounds of strangers, sighs, coughs, cries. And from one nearby room, farts so loud and varied it was like a party gag.

Ben smiled, even semi-conscious.

A doctor he hadn't seen—or couldn't remember seeing—bent and peered into his eyes.

"Good, you're coming around. Still unevenly dilated, though."

"Is this where I say *where am I?*" Ben asked.

The doctor, a wiry man wearing a knee-length white lab coat and dark toupee that sat atop his graying fringe like a lamb chop, straightened and looked at him.

"You tell me."

Ben scanned the little room.

"Hospital? 'Course, that's just a guess." He felt an exorbitant amount of gauze around his skull. "What's beneath this bandage?"

"A wound. Some staples. A concussion. You remember?"

Ben rummaged through his memory. "Sort of. Where's the wound?"

"Crown. Won't ruin your looks."

"How long have I been here? How'd I get here?"

"Ambulance."

"I mean—"

"Nine-one-one."

"When can I leave?"

"Not yet."

"I was with another officer last night. Jack Malone. Is he OK?"

"I don't know anything about that."

"I need to make a call."

"In a while. For now, you need to rest."

"What'd I get hit with?"

"Something heavy."

#

They continued to wake Ben every couple of hours until noon, then a nurse with mocha skin and molasses in her voice came in, busied herself with pulse, pressure, and temperature, and said *sleep now.*

When he next woke, it was to go to the john. He eased himself off the edge of the bed and assessed his condition. Balance tricky. In the bathroom, he stood at the toilet with one hand on the wall. He washed his hands, then peered under the bandage across the wound on his knuckles. The stitches looked OK. He looked at himself in the mirror—head swathed in bandage and purple deltas of hemorrhage beneath both eyes.

The nurse with the mocha skin pulled the bathroom door all the way open and looked in.

"What you doin' up?" she asked, her honeyed voice reproachful. She took him firmly by the forearm and led him back into the room, to the bed, held onto him as he lay down.

"Don't be gettin' up, hear?" she said sternly and pointed to a call button on his bed rail. "Press that button, somebody come runnin.' "

"Nurse Ratched," Ben said.

She fluffed his pillow and fixed him with eyes the color and shine of chestnuts.

"Believe it, darlin'," she said. "That make you the cuckoo."

She smelled like soap and shampoo and toothpaste.

"You smell good," Ben said.

"Don't go trying to make up."

She gently lifted his eyelids, checked his pupils, wrote something on his chart.

"You had visitors. Said they'd come back."

"Who?"

"Family, I reckon. Both tall, like you. Dark-haired woman, white-haired man."

Right. Dayton was in town.

Bood.

He tried to sit up, and she restrained him.

"I have to take care of my dog."

"He's seen to. Your visitors said to tell you that."

He lay back, relieved, and the nurse gave his sheets a tug.

"The verb *bustle* was invented to describe nurses," he said.

She ran a long hand over her cap of graying frizz and headed for the door.

"Only bustle I know is the one behind me."

From where he lay, Ben could see through the window a column of red crape myrtles marching across the landscape, stirring in the breeze, foreshortened shadows lying to their east. The wall clock read two o'clock.

Twelve hours since the Texas Toast. Someone waiting on the porch—for Malone, or for him?

Shatto. He pressed the call button, and Nurse Ratched answered.

"Where's my stuff?" Ben asked.

"What stuff, darlin'?"

"Cell phone. Wallet. Watch. Clothes."

"Your clothes are in that little closet next to the bathroom. Other stuff in the drawer in the bedstand. Don't get up. I'll be right down."

Ben cautiously eased himself into a sitting position and put his legs over the edge of the bed. Testing his equilibrium, he braced an extended hand against the bedstand and leaned to open the little drawer. It held two items: a bible and a badge.

He pressed the call button again.

Nurse Ratched said, "You gonna be high maintenance, I can tell."

"Where's my cell phone? There's nothing in this drawer but a fuckin' bible and my badge."

Stolen last night, of course. No surprise there. But *shit!*

"Well, all I can say to you before you get even nastier is whatever's in the drawer is what you got."

"So my wallet's gone. My driver's license and credit cards. Cell phone. Money. My watch. Aw, shit, my watch!"

The Blums' gift to him all those years ago.

"Look like it, baby. Think maybe that's why they hit you on the head?"

Ben let loose a stream of profanity.

"I'm on my way down there," Ratched said soothingly. "Any minute now."

"Great. Can I get a smaller headdress?"

"No."

"Can I get out of here?"

"No."

"Can I get something for my black eyes?"

"Like what?"

"Hell, I don't know. You're the nurse. An icepack?"

"You just relax, and I'll be right down, darlin'."

Ben fell asleep waiting for the icepack, and the next time he woke up, Malone was in the room. He closed his eyes again, without speaking, and turned his face to the wall—sensing rather than seeing Malone approach the bed.

After a while, Malone said, "I know you're awake."

Ben stared into the red-black nothingness of his closed eyelids.

"I can see your eyelids flickering," Malone added.

Ben lay still and silent for a moment. Then, fumbling for the call button, he gave it a push.

Ratched answered with a sigh.

"Nurse," Ben said. "Please come to my room at once and wake me up. I'm having a nightmare."

"Very funny," Malone said.

"You want a nightmare," Ratched said, "keep pushin' on that button."

Ben turned his head on the pillow and looked at Malone. "You look like hell."

The detective swiped a freckled paw across his nostrils. "So do you."

Ben sat up—too quickly, because it felt like his brain rocked in his cranium. He waited for the room to steady before he spoke.

"Last night, Jack," he said, biting down hard on the words but trying to remain deliberate and calm, "last night I was asleep in my bed and some guy I've never met called me and said you were in trouble. Now why should this concern me? I don't know. But concern me it did. So I got out of bed and dressed and drove to a sad bar in a sad part of town and found you sitting drunk and stoned on the curb. So I took you to your place, where an anvil dropped on my head."

He took a deep breath, let it out easy.

"Thing is, Jack, I don't know what's real anymore where you're concerned. Did you set me up?"

"Ah, Christ—"

"*Did* you set me up? I honest-to-god don't know. And that mournful look on your face right now, Jacko. Is that real?"

"You're a self-righteous sonsabitch, aren't you."

"Probably. But I'm not dirty."

Malone's small, knowing smile infuriated Ben.

"All those choices you made along the line, Jack? You made them. There's not a cop alive who doesn't know how it works. A little at a time. And when you finally look around and see where you are, you're far from where you meant to go. But there's no way back."

Malone reddened. "I was doing this job—and doing it well—before you were even born, kiddo. And I gave it everything. I lost my wife. My kids. My house. I'd say my *life*, except my life was this, this fucking job."

Ben gritted his teeth. "Hang on—I'll get my violin."

It seemed to Ben that Malone winced. He sighed.

179

"All that, Jack—yeah. Those are the reasons you're still on the force. Those are the reasons people like you paralyze people like me."

Resolve abruptly struck Ben across the chest like an iron bar. No more.

"Jack. Listen. Fair warning. I'm documenting your shit. You're old enough for early retirement. I'm saying take it. Otherwise, I'm sharing what I know, and you'll go down. But first, you'll be swallowed up in the protocol you hate so much. And unless you're fuckin' lucky, swallowed up by the press you hate so much. Maybe you'll even have to kiss your pension goodbye—"

Malone turned away.

"Remember, Jack," Ben said, raising his volume. "Protocol, press, pension. Three P's. All that alliteration. Should be easy to keep in mind."

Malone moved toward the door, but Ben couldn't leave it alone.

"You still got a choice, Jack."

Malone reached the doorway just as Nurse Ratched hustled in from the corridor, rubber soles squeaking on the waxed tile.

"What's going on?" she asked. "I can hear you all the way to the desk."

"Get that man out of here," Ben told her. "He's disturbing the patient."

"I'm gone," Malone said.

"And you," Ratched said, fixing Ben with her red-brown eyes. "You're disturbing the peace. You want me to call the police?"

She poured a glass of water and handed him a tiny pleated cup containing an oval tablet, stood there while he tossed the pill into his mouth and swallowed it with a large draft of water.

"I hope that's cyanide," he muttered.

She gave his pillow and bedding a couple slaps and picked up the dinner menu from his bedside table, thrust it into his hand.

"Mark your choices, give you something to do besides cause trouble."

When she left the room, he pulled over the wheeled tray, turned the menu over to its blank side, picked up the pencil from the bedside table, and stared into the middle distance for a time. He was worried about Shatto, about the questions he wanted answered. But he found himself sketching Nurse Ratched, the broad forehead and close-cropped nap that covered her skull, the chestnut-colored eyes and high wide cheekbones. A sturdy brown woman Gauguin might have painted. Or Diego Rivera. He worked quickly, taking the sketch down to her collarbones with thick strokes—then, with the flat side of the pencil lead, shaded the rest into nothing.

He held up the drawing and examined it. The light came through the pale paper, and some of the menu's offerings were written backwards across Nurse Ratched's face.

CHAPTER TWENTY-NINE

Saturday afternoon, August 25

Ben awoke to a dinner he hadn't ordered and didn't want. What he wanted was to get out of here and talk to Shatto. Resolving never to take another of Nurse Ratched's little oval pills, he pulled himself into a sitting position but lay back when he heard movement in the hall.

Incredibly, Jack Malone came striding in again, a creased paper bag in his hand.

Ben groaned.

"You've got to be kidding."

"Hang on," Malone said. "Just hang on."

He emptied the contents of the bag onto the bed. Displaying the items to Ben one by one, he laid them in the drawer beside Ben's badge. Wallet. Cell phone. Watch.

"Hand me the watch," Ben said. Malone dropped it into his outstretched hand, and Ben studied it. It looked fine, tiny second hand ticking away the tiny seconds.

His phone still had some juice, and he was relieved to see Shatto hadn't tried to call. But if he had, Ben at least would have a callback number. Wait—Shatto's call last night. That number would be in Ben's home phone.

"How did you get this stuff back?"

"I have friends as well as enemies," Malone said. "Couple of assholes thought it would be cool to roll a cop. They were after me. Your dough is gone. But there's your wallet, driver's license, credit cards. Phone and watch. And here are your car keys. I took your car over to your place, left it

locked up in the drive. Wouldn't be safe in my neighborhood."

"As though it never happened, eh, Jack?"

"I got help, didn't I? Soon's I saw what was goin' down?
Called nine-one-one. Got your stuff back. Also, I got the
names of the five guys at Jiggy Ruben's poker game. Six,
counting Jiggy."

He handed Ben a folded sheet of paper, and Ben opened
it. Six names, printed in Malone's sprawling hand. Jiggy
Ruben. Lonnie Lacefield. LeRoy Shatto.

"Numbers four and five are high rollers," Malone said. "I
don't know that last guy."

John Cheek.

"I do," Ben said.

Malone put an appeal into his colorless little eyes, but
Ben didn't have anything left to give. The final dregs of his
affection for his old partner had drained away.

"Jack," Ben said. "Don't. Yes, you got my stuff back. But
this placating shit, as though it could make everything
OK—it's like bragging that the Titanic took longer to sink
than the Lusitania."

Malone made an unreadable gesture.

"Point is," Ben said, "the Titanic still sank."

#

In the tiny bathroom, Ben slipped on the black pullover
and chinos he'd worn to the Texas Toast, pushed his feet
into his sandals and, holding on to a steel support bar, faced
himself in the mirror. The news wasn't good. A pallid man
wearing two days of stubble, a huge white turban of gauze,
and two fiercely black eyes. He loosened the tape from the

nape of his neck and started unwinding the gauze. Kept on till he had a pile of the white stuff in the sink. Soon the shape of his head emerged, and he unwound some more. He wished he could see the top of his head. Surely there was some small central dressing under all this bandage, protecting the wound and staples. His hair emerged from beneath the gauze, but it didn't look much like hair—more like flattened wads of tar.

By lowering his chin and looking out the tops of his eyes—which were swollen to mere slits—he could see a bit of the shaved place on his crown and a square dressing. He didn't want to risk the dressing's sterility by dampening his hair, so he left it.

He'd liked Nurse Ratched. Too bad he couldn't stick around to say goodbye. He moved to the nightstand and, picking up the menu with Ratched's likeness on the back, laid it on the pillow, sketch side up. Then he went into the corridor, looked around, entered the stairwell and, holding onto the banister, started down. Passed a couple of hospital workers on their way up, too deep in conversation to pay any attention to him. On the ground floor, he left the stairwell, crossed the lobby, and went out the main door.

Where he stopped short. He had car keys but no car.

Fine. How far was home—two miles? He stood a moment longer, assessing his strength, then strode out of the hospital drive and walked west on Randol Mill.

#

When he got home, he greeted the ecstatic Bood and left a message for Nell that he was home. Then he scrolled through his phone calls and pressed the callback button for L. Shatto.

No answer. He listened for the beep and said, "LeRoy, you know who this is. Where are you? I'm waiting for your call."

Then, head pounding and legs throbbing from his long trek, he undressed, closed his blinds against the light, and fell into bed.

The chief woke him.

"Sorry to call on Sunday," he said, and even dazed with sleep, Ben smiled slightly at his rote civility. Fact was, Rolando Saenz never minded calling any moment or any day. What he *minded* was that every single member of the force was not on duty twenty-four-seven.

Wait, Ben thought. *Sunday?* A thin gray light filtered around the shades. Dusk or dawn?

"I knew you'd want to know," the chief was saying. "LeRoy Shatto."

Ben sat up—too suddenly, because for a millisecond, everything went black.

"First responders are still there," the chief added. "Team's on the way. You might want to take a look before they bag the body. You gonna roust Malone? Or do you want me to?"

"I'll do it," said Ben, thinking: *Roust Malone? No fucking way.*

CHAPTER THIRTY

Sunday, August 26

Ben pulled into the Starbuck lot on Fielder, where Hilda Cloy waited, holding two tall cups. Handing Ben the coffee, she jumped in and snapped her squat body under the seatbelt, taking back one of the cups as Ben made a tight, one-handed turn back onto Fielder and swung east on I-30.

#

They pushed through the gaggle of media in front of LeRoy Shatto's ramshackle apartment building and mounted the narrow stairs to Shatto's third-floor apartment, the open door strung across with precautionary yellow crime scene tape. An officer was stationed at the door, holding a clipboard. Ben and Hilda scribbled their initials and badge numbers on the hand-drawn lines of the sign-in sheet and ducked under the tape.

Inside, the first person they saw—to Ben's disappointment—was Malone, his colorless hair combed flat and the slack skin beneath his eyes dark as coffee stains. He gave Ben an accusing glance that said *your partner has to get his call-out from the police radio?*

The other investigators were collecting trace evidence, dusting, measuring, photographing. They looked up briefly but said nothing. The apartment reeked with the stench of death, a smell that to Ben seemed a sort of foul metallic odor mixed with the stink of spoiled meat.

Shatto lay naked in his bathtub behind a stained blue shower curtain printed all over in white seashells. The stink was stronger in this small, hot, filthy room, and the air was thick with flies—their collective buzz louder somehow than the sounds of the investigators in the other rooms. Ben pushed aside the shower curtain with a gloved hand. Shatto lay with knees sharply bent and resting against the tub's sides, big hands quiet at last beside his lean torso, the once-restless amber eyes unmoving, long feet flat against the tub's bottom. The porcelain was smeared with bloodstains the browned-red of burnt transmission fluid.

Ben registered his own sweat-damp clothing and the shock of seeing someone he'd known in life in this eternal state of stillness. The gorge rose in his throat, and he pushed it down. He pointed to the gaping, dark-edged gashes crossing the dead man's wrists and inner thighs, and Hilda and Malone crowded close.

"Aww," Hilda said, turning away. "Why'd he do that to himself?"

"He didn't," Malone said.

Ben saw in Malone a hint of his old self—and of his talent for immediately sizing up a situation. Ben leaned in to scrutinize the body, took his time. The drain held an old-fashioned rubber plug connected to a chain, but the tub was empty.

"Tub had water in it," Ben said. "But not now."

"Plug doesn't fit," Malone said. "The water washed away a lot of the blood and stench, though."

"But not all," Hilda said, her face as long and mournful as a Modigliani sketch.

"Who found the body?" Ben asked Malone, who was rummaging in a nightstand drawer with a gloved hand.

When he didn't respond, Ben went looking for Charlaine Clayton, whom he'd seen in the living room. He returned to find Hilda still with Shatto's body, as if sitting shiva, a tissue over her mouth and nose, face shining with sweat and a patch of wet between her shoulder blades.

"Charlaine said the maid found him," Ben said.

Malone glanced around the filthy room, his glacial eyes incredulous.

"Maid?"

"Well, whoever. Landlady, probably." Ben looked around. "I've seen enough. They can bag it."

"I'll stay a bit," Malone said. "See what the investigating officers have to say."

Ben gazed at his partner for a millisecond, then nodded.

Outside, he and Hilda settled themselves in the Lexus, and headed for I-30.

"So . . . not suicide," Hilda said.

"Bathtub suicides are tricky. The three such so-called suicides I've seen were all actually homicides. Same thing—victim nude in the tub."

"So?"

"Suicides who do a blood-letting in a bathtub are in the tub because they don't want to make a mess. They're usually clothed."

"They'd rather not be found naked? God. As if it made a difference."

"As if. But it's force of habit. Like when people jump. They take off their glasses first. Put them in a pocket, leave them on the window sill or rooftop or bridge. They're not really thinking. Consider their emotional state. What might make sense to a suicide might not make sense to us. Or to the killer. He thinks: My vic's in the tub, so I better get his clothes off. That's rational, but suicide is irrational."

"Also, LeRoy didn't have any test cuts."

Ben agreed.

"Nothing but four decisive gashes. All the suicides I've worked showed hesitation cuts—small and shallow cuts on the wrists or torso. Trying to get up the courage. They're not like defensive wounds, which appear on the palms or dorsal sides of the arms. Victim protecting himself. We'll see what the M.E. says, but I think LeRoy was drugged before they put him in the tub. Something like rohypnol."

"Roofies," Hilda said.

"Or GHB or ketamine. The result is the same, especially with alcohol. In half an hour, he's incapacitated."

"Or unconscious."

"Depending on how much he got. My guess is he was in a situation he'd been in any number of times—a friendly little high with buddies and a handful of pills. It'd be easy to slip him something."

"So he's incapacitated. Still, if they wanted to pass it off as suicide . . . wouldn't they know the drug would show up in the autopsy?"

"They'd reason he could have taken it himself—for the high. Plenty of people do. Anyway, most thugs and criminals are stupid—you ever noticed?"

Ben got on the ramp to I-30 and drove the short distance to Fielder and Starbucks.

"LeRoy called me Friday night," he said. "He wanted to talk. We planned a meet yesterday."

He touched the bandage on his head. "Then *this* happened."

She waited.

Pointing a thumb in the direction of Shatto's apartment, he added, "Then *that* happened."

"Someone didn't want him talking to you."

"Malone claims the guy on his porch and Shatto's so-called suicide are not connected."

"What do you think?"

"I don't know, Hilda. Honest to god."

She said nothing, and Ben glanced at her. Her cratered cheek was turned away. They were silent until he pulled up beside her parked car and she opened the door and slid out. Then she bent and poked her head back inside, her expression cheerless.

"I liked him, boss. Shatto."

When he got home, Ben opened a bottle of red. And drank it all.

CHAPTER THIRTY-ONE

Monday morning, August 27

Ben woke with a clanging head and a mouth like the bottom of a birdcage. He shambled to the bathroom and stared into the mirror, his only thought that he could pass for a raccoon.

He tugged the dressing from his scalp, which looked more and more like a monk's tonsure, and stepped into the shower. The water was hot and delicious.

"Ahhh," he groaned. He shampooed gingerly, scrubbed, and stepped on the bath mat.

And the phone rang. Six-forty in the morning? His heart both sank and quickened when he saw Slydell Scroggins' name on caller ID.

Monday.

"Don't say it," he told Sly.

"Another note."

"What's it say?"

"I didn't open it."

God almighty.

"Open it, Sly."

"Forensics—"

"Slit the envelope along the bottom and slip out the note. Christ, Sly, you know how to avoid disturbing DNA."

He heard the paper rustling in Sly's hands.

"It says . . . not sure how to pronounce it. Oelander." Sly spelled it. "Deceased August 27. Then there's a quote. 'Mother is in the attic. She was too heavy to move.' "

Ben frowned.

"That rings a bell. Spell that name again."

"O-e-l-a-n-d-e-r."

"Hang on." Ben sprinted into the bedroom, pulled a phone book from a shelf, and picked up the bedside phone.

"One Oelander in the Arlington directory," he told Sly. "Canterbury Lane—720 Canterbury Lane."

He knew the street—off South Bowen, little before I-20. *Oelander, Theodore*, the entry said, and beneath that, indented: *Bonnie, Katie, Teddy, Troy*.

"Call this number, Sly. But stay on with me." He read the Oelanders' number.

Sly hit the conference call button and punched in the number. It rang. And rang. Then it went to the recorder, and Ben heard a woman's clear and musical voice, a voice with a hint of a smile: *Hello! You've reached the Oelanders . . . .*

No answer? Early in the morning on the second week of school, three school-age kids, and no answer? Where were Ted and Bonnie Oelander? Where were Katie, Teddy, and Troy?

"Goddammit! Call Kenechi, Sly. Tell him to pick me up. And get backup to the Canterbury address. We might need a warrant. I'll call the chief."

He shrugged into a shirt, pushed his feet into trousers, a pair of loafers. Strapped on his Glock, grabbed his jacket, keys, wallet, and cell phone. Shook some kibbles into Bood's dish, refilled his water. Then he was down the corridor toward the garage, sending a dismissive wave in the direction of the security alarm panel. The last thing he saw as he closed the door was Bood, looking up at him with a mixture of concern and disappointment.

Ben called the chief and paced back and forth until Kenechi's unmarked steamed into the cul de sac and hurled itself up the drive, its magnetic blue light flashing. The car lurched to a halt only long enough for Ben to jump in.

Arlington's rush hour wouldn't have started yet. At this speed, ten minutes to Canterbury. Fifteen at most. But, flying through the intersections, Ben thought: *It doesn't matter how fast we get there if it's already too late.*

If the killer followed his pattern.

"Kenechi," Ben said. "Mother is in the attic. She was too heavy to move. Ring any bells?"

The radio spit out Sly's voice.

"Your team's on the way. Couldn't raise Malone. I'll keep—"

"Don't worry about Malone."

"Four uniforms pretty close. Coy and Charlaine on Matlock. Pearl and Hanna on I-20."

Ben grabbed the mike. "We need a quiet approach, Sly. When they get close to 720, they should park out of sight. Tell them to wait if they get there before we do."

#

Ben saw a couple of cruisers sitting in the shade when they pulled into Canterbury Lane. Charlaine and Coy were in the first cruiser, and a little farther, under a large live oak, sat Pearl and Hanna. Around a little bend, up a rise and down again, was 720. Kenechi pulled the magnetic flasher off the rooftop, and he and Ben coasted by, rubbernecking. The house was a big two-story colonial, white with blue shutters, well back from the street, suitable for a family with a little girl and two little boys. They drove out of sight, made a U-turn and drove back, nice and slow. Attached three-car garage, doors down. Large American flag furled and leaning against the garage, beside the door, as though someone meant to put it inside and forgot. A doghouse out back, no dog.

Just after the bend, a wide lane led up another little rise, out of sight. Now Hilda and Proudhorse also waited behind the cruisers, with Pratt and Naldo just swinging around the corner. Kenechi turned around again, and Ben lowered the window and put out a beckoning arm. They all pulled into the wide lane, flashers and sirens off, everybody getting out, nobody slamming doors.

"Might be best if we just go over this little rise, approach that way," Ben told them. "No place to park near the house without being in plain view. Everything looks quiet, but . . . Coy, you and Charlaine check out the front, and Pearl and Hanna, the back. Hilda, Proudhorse, back them up, but stay out of sight—maybe in that little stand of trees." He pointed to an outcropping to the northwest of the house. "Pratt and Naldo, you too. Get as close as you can and still be out of sight. Soon as you've had a look, come back and we'll reconnoiter."

They slipped on ballistic vests and helmets and checked their shoulder mikes.

Ben and Kenechi positioned themselves to watch.

Nothing happened. Ben shielded his eyes against the early sun, the sky as cloudless as if it had been washed. The Oelanders' wide porch was shaded by a pillared portico and fronted with bronze-red azaleas. A rosemary plant cast its fragrance on the air, and the breeze stirred scarlet-throated hibiscus the color of marigolds. Ben didn't paint flowers, but if he did, that hibiscus would be the flower he'd paint. He

194

saw that the sprinklers had been on—the drive wore two half-moons of damp, and birds pecked at the wet grass. A large crow cawed loudly from the roof's highest peak, and two irritated sparrows nesting beneath the eaves flew up and attacked him. Wings widespread, the crow launched himself off the roof and landed among some black brethren, who opened their long beaks in unison to curse the sparrows.

A man walking a yellow lab on the sidewalk started toward them, and Ben stopped him with a raised hand.

"Get that guy out of here," he told Kenechi.

Pearl and Hanna were at the edge of a large expanse of lawn at the rear of 720, Coy and Charlaine at the front. Stationed at the house's four corners, the officers waited for a second, listening. Charlaine looked up the rise toward Ben, hauled up her shoulders in an exaggerated shrug, and spoke into her shoulder.

"I hear organ music," her voice sputtered. "Church music. Really loud, too."

Ben froze. "John List."

"Come again?" said Charlaine.

Ben turned toward the sidewalk, where Kenechi was banishing the man with the yellow lab.

"Who's John List?" Charlaine repeated, her voice laced with static.

Ben stood rooted as the uniformed cops sidled near the Oelanders' windows, peered cautiously inside, and ran back through the wooded area toward Ben.

A breathless Charlaine reached him first.

"Music's pretty freaky."

"And loud," said Coy. "Up close, you can feel its vibrations."

"Otherwise nothing and nobody," Charlaine said.

"What was that old true crime TV show?" Ben asked abruptly. "With that guy Walsh?"

"America's Most Wanted?" Charlaine asked.

"That's it," Ben said.

Kenechi mounted the rise, and Ben turned.

"Ken."

The urgency in Ben's voice brought Kenechi to a standstill on the rise.

"John List," Ben said.

"Oh, my god."

CHAPTER THIRTY-TWO

"The Oelanders aren't home, Ben," Kenechi said. "According to that guy."

He tipped his head toward the man with the yellow lab.

"A neighbor. Dave Asquith. Says the Oelanders are on vacation. That's their dog—he's watching it for them."

"Vacation?"

"Something queered their plans, but they'd already paid for a bunch of it and decided to go themselves, leave the kids with their aunt so they could go to school." He took out his notebook. "I've got the aunt's contact info."

"I hope to god . . . ." Ben looked down at the Oelander place.

"Who is John List?" Charlaine asked again.

"You don't remember that sicko?" Proudhorse asked. "Guess you're too young."

"Religious nut," Ben said. "Murdered his whole family— wife, three children, mother. Shooting spree in the family mansion."

"Playing church music on the intercom the whole time," Joe Proudhorse said. "Still playing when the police came, days later."

"What happened to him?" Charlaine asked.

"Got clean away, and made a new life for himself as someone else," Ben said. "Then eighteen, twenty years later, that TV show reprised the case and someone recognized List's pictures, turned him in."

"So that's our copycat case," Hilda said.

"John List had a wife and three children," Ben said. "A girl and two boys, and they all were murdered. Theodore Oelander also has a wife and three children, a girl and two boys."

"Could they be in there?" asked Charlaine. Her cheeks, always pale, looked white next to her coppery hair.

"Someone set up that organ music," Ben said. "We're going in. The back door," he asked Pearl and Hanna. "Wood?"

"Steel."

"Let's breach the front door. It's wood, double, probably a deadbolt. Something fast. And try the door first to see if it's unlocked," he added, expecting them to say *duh*. They didn't—maybe recalling, like Ben, police breaking down unlocked doors.

"We have a metal SWAT ram. Two-man," Charlaine said.

"OK. Pearl and Hanna, use the ram. Charlaine and Coy, first in, Pearl and Hanna backing up. Hilda, Proudhorse, watch the back. Pratt, Naldo, the sides. Wait till Kenechi and I are set, in case someone gets out another way."

Before the word *go* was out of Ben's mouth, adrenalin scattered the team, the detectives running silently, the uniforms chinking and clinking as they jogged away carrying their weapons. Ben let them get in place—Hilda and Proudhorse at the back, Pratt and Naldo at each side. Pearl and Hanna waited, ram poised, ready to joust with the double doors, Charlaine and Coy at their sides, swat rifles ready at their shoulders.

Ben dropped a hand, and Charlaine stepped quickly to the door, tried the knob and sent a thumb's down in Ben and Kenechi's direction. Pearl and Hanna plunged toward the door, wood splintering. Backed up and took another run.

The door heaved inward with the second thrust and in the instant of silence that followed, as if the world hung on a breath, there was a sound like a gust of wind, then the whoosh of a huge fireball as tall as a man, its colors bright and bizarre. The fireball splintered the doors and spiraled out of sight on a tail of white smoke, followed immediately by a deafening explosion, the front of the house flying away, the four uniformed officers vanishing among shards and slabs and timber.

Ben and Kenechi, frozen for the instant of the fireball, half-ran, half-fell down the hill, the percussion of the explosion stopping them in their tracks and laying them flat. Now they were up and racing toward what had been the pillared portico—Pratt and Naldo and Hilda and Proudhorse running, too. The front of the house was shorn away by the explosion—the entry now a flame-filled cavity, the rooms behind like a cutaway model, everything smoking.

Ben stumbled over the hot debris, ears resounding with white noise from the explosion. He ran to and fro over the rubble, screaming, unable to hear his own voice. *Charlaine! Coy! Pearl! Hanna!* He saw Kenechi peering into the flames of the cutaway rooms then dashing toward him, his lips moving soundlessly. Hilda and Proudhorse were lurching in circles, Pratt and Naldo still now, looking at Ben uncomprehendingly.

Beneath the edge of a smoking slab, Ben saw a blackened limb and grabbed the large hunk with his bare hands, searing his palms. He dropped it—but not before he saw Charlaine Clayton's shapely arm, wearing only a Swiss

Army watch and a splayed hand with immaculately lacquered nails. Ben turned, tried to hold steady, to absorb the shock, his knees like water and stomach heaving. Charlaine Clayton, a Beautiful One, lying dismembered among debris like just more debris. Leaning against a beam, Ben was aware of its heat through his shirt, then of strong hands on his shoulders. Kenechi, black face frosted with ash, was speaking. Ben saw his lips move but heard only a sound like the beating of wings. Now Kenechi shouted, Ben's right ear vibrating like a muted drum, picking up a little sound.

Ben raised a hand to touch the dressing on his head. It wasn't there—he felt only staples and stiffened hair. He put his hands over his ears. Kenechi was fumbling with a two-by-four, and Ben realized vaguely that he was trying to pry the smoking slab off Charlaine's arm. His swirling head steadied for an instant, and he gaped at the scene around him as if seeing it for the first time. Pratt and Naldo still stood like pillars, but Hilda and Proudhorse were moving toward him, their expressions a study in horror and disbelief.

"Ben!" Kenechi grabbed his arm. "Get help! I can do this!"

Ben heard the words as if from a great distance. In another circumstance, Ben might ponder the role reversal—Kenechi leading. But in the moment, he understood Kenechi's *I can do this*; civil war had shown him smoking corpses and dismembered body parts.

He sprang to life and sprinted for the car radio.

#

The bomb squad disabled a second homemade device
rigged to the back door through a hubbub of ambulance, fire
engine, babbling press corps, and TV news helicopters.

After the explosion, astonished neighbors had assembled
on the sidewalk in front of the house—including the man
with the yellow lab.

"Yeah," Dave Asquith told Ben. "They're taking their RV
up to Idaho, through the Coeur d'Alene area. They usually
take Charlie, but they had some side trips—"

"Who's Charlie?"

Asquith looked at the dog.

"When did they leave?" Ben asked.

"Friday."

"You're sure of that?"

Asquith drew back a little, a man with military bearing
and a freshly clipped brush of white mustache.

"Of course I'm sure of it. I watched them go. I have their
dog. You want Ted's cell number?"

"I do."

#

Now, after the bomb squad and ambulances and fire
engines and water hoses and body bags and investigators
and reports, Kenechi and Ben headed north on Fielder,
Hilda following in an unmarked, Kenechi driving because
Ben's hands were encased in gauze mitts.

Turned out Ted and Bonnie Oelander were fine—at least
as fine as you can be when you learn your house has blown
up. So were the kids—Katie, Teddy, and Troy. Even Charlie
the dog was fine.

But Charlaine Clayton and Coy Ellis were not fine. And

Pearl and Hanna were not fine. They were dead, Hanna four months from retirement.

Ben's gut clenched.

The Oelanders were returning—Ted would fly, Bonnie would make the two-day drive in the RV. Ben would talk to Ted Oelander tomorrow. He'd find the connections. The killer knew the Oelanders—knew they'd be gone, knew when they were leaving, knew all about it. He'd had his template case and his matching victims, but he hadn't killed them. He'd set a trap for the police instead. Set a trap for Ben. But it was Charlaine and Coy and Pearl and Hanna who got caught.

Kenechi worked his way north through the afternoon traffic while Ben stared unseeing through the passenger window, his ears still muted as if filled with cotton batting, the city and its routine activity surreal. His bandaged hands lay useless in his lap, the dressings out of proportion to the damage done. Five minutes inside his door, this bulk of gauze and tape would be in his wastebasket, and he'd be on his way to the office.

He turned to say so to Kenechi, who drove silently, eyes on the windshield, tears carving a tiny rivulet through soot and grease and running over the crescent of scar on his cheek.

Ben looked away.

Kenechi pulled into Ben's garage and climbed out.

"I'm OK," Ben said, shoving the door open and clambering from the car. Kenechi put out his big fists, and Ben touched them with his own giant mitts. Like boxers before a fight. Then Kenechi ducked beneath the garage door and headed to where Hilda waited in the unmarked, motor running, her face gray behind the glass.

#

Ben waited at the door to his kitchen while the garage door descended, his bandaged mitt on the knob. He heard the frenzied snuffling at the crack of the door, the dance of toenails against hardwood on the other side. *Sit* and *stay* meant nothing at homecoming. Bood had once greeted Ben by jumping up and down so frantically that he'd displaced a kneecap on a hind leg, a mishap the vet called a luxating patella and that had required surgery. Now, Ben's practice was to grab Bood mid-jump—he was more successful catching him in midair than he was keeping him from jumping.

The complication was that Ben not only had to seize Bood, he also had to turn off the security system. Then he remembered. He hadn't set the alarm in his rush to get out of the house this morning.

He tapped the door and said, "Hey, Bood."

From the other side of the door came a yelp tinged with hysteria. Bracing himself, Ben pushed the door open to a tumult of spring-loaded leaps that brought the dog almost level with Ben's nose. Ben caught him clumsily at the apex of a high jump, Bood instantly noticing his bandaged hands and aiming his black gaze at Ben like an accusation.

"I think you're turning into Ma, Bood," Ben said.

In the bathroom, Ben removed the gauze dressings. His whole body felt numb—except for his hands, which throbbed with every heartbeat—but he was almost grateful for the pain. He examined the burns. His swollen palms were an archipelago of blisters that protected the damaged flesh beneath. Later, he'd cover the blisters, but for now, it felt better to have nothing on them.

He didn't go to the office. Instead, he sat at the computer, called up a search engine, and tapped out "john list" with one index finger. There was no shortage of history on the case. He read everything, printing certain passages, then went into the bedroom and fell across the bed, face down. Bood joined him, licking his cheek, sniffing the strange smells on his clothing, curious about his hands and, finally, settling beside him, aligning the curve of his small body to Ben's.

But Ben was too restless to sleep, and eventually he rose, stripped, and got into the shower, where he stood in a stream of hot water—holding his burned hands out of the flow. He got out and stood in the center of the room, zombie-like, remembering this morning in this very spot, trailing water over the marble floor to take the call that would cost the lives of four people. This morning. It was like another life. A happier, blessed life—when Charlaine Clayton and Coy Ellis and Tyler Pearl and Lyle Hanna were alive. Driving along in their squad cars south of town, good cops doing their jobs—as innocent and pitiful as anyone who is about to die.

The phone rang. He didn't get up, but let it go to the recording.

"Benny," Nell said. "Pick up. Kenechi called. I need to know you're OK."

Ben took up the receiver.

"I'm OK, Ma."

"I'm coming over."

"No, Ma. I'm OK, but I'm wiped out."

When they'd hung up, Ben pulled on his pajama pants and went to the kitchen. He opened the refrigerator door, looked around inside, and shoved it closed. Took a bottle of red from the wine rack, opened it, poured a glass and drank it standing by the sink.

"What the hell," he breathed.

Lying like bright beads of blood against the porcelain of the sink were scarlet petals and a few stem cuttings. He stared an instant longer, picking up one velvety petal and tossing it back into the sink . . . and rushed through the house, peering into every room, Bood hard on his heels.

Nothing. Nobody. Of course.

He went back to the kitchen and poured another glass of wine. He should call the chief. Someone had been in his house and wanted him to know. Ben's eye fell on the French door that led to the patio. Did he unlock that door this morning to let Bood out, or had Bood used his doggy door? He strode to the door and tried the knob. It was locked, but the deadbolt wasn't in place. He turned on the patio light, stepped out onto the flagstones, and took a little tour of the patio and his back garden. He went back inside and pulled the door closed, flipping the lever to secure the deadbolt.

Tomorrow would be soon enough to tell the chief.

He downed his wine, poured another, and headed for the bathroom. On the way, he surveyed his living room again, flipping on the overhead light, which also started the ceiling fan rotating slowly, eerily.

And there they were. Perfectly arranged in his own gleaming crystal vase, perfectly centered on his cocktail table. Red, red roses. He bent to pluck the little white card from the bouquet, checked the motion, and instead cocked his head to read a single short line, printed in block letters and black marker.

A charmed life, it said.

He stared at the card. Forensics would need it . . . .

Tomorrow would be soon enough for that, too.

In the bathroom, he took a vial of pain pills from the medicine chest—the strong ones, for his back. The pills that knocked him out and that he shouldn't combine with alcohol. He shook a capsule into his burned palm and washed it down with wine.

Minutes later, he was beneath the sheet, drifting on booze and pills, thinking, *that's how it starts.* And his last thoughts, before he slept, were of Malone.

CHAPTER THIRTY-THREE

Tuesday, August 28

What he noticed at the office next morning was the silence. He nodded at the desk sergeant when he entered the building, and the sergeant nodded back. He handed off his Glock and the stuff in his pockets, stepped through the metal detector, and retrieved his belongings, all without speaking or being spoken to.

Same thing in the squad room. Sly handed Ben some messages and Ben, in his turn, handed Sly the three-page printout he'd made the night before. A sticky note on the top said: *Need copies.* Sly took the printouts and turned away without a word.

Same thing in the conference room—usually a hubbub. Kenechi, as usual, was polished and smelled of soap and talc and aftershave. But his face was creased and swollen. Hilda's downcast eyes were puffy. Proudhorse sat stoic, his dark gaze fixed on something in the middle distance. Pratt's fleshy face was in his hands, and Naldo was not fidgeting for once, but immobile and expressionless. Only Malone was out of his chair, moving in tight circles around the room as if working off excess energy, his freckled hands busy and face fierce and red.

To Ben's surprise, the chief was in place against the windows, blinds drawn against the sun. No rushing in late this morning. Saenz's black hair was gelled and shining, but his shirt and blazer seemed thrown on and his face, like Kenechi's, had the mangled look of a sleepless night.

Saenz watched Ben come in and take his seat, looked at his hands and tonsured, bandaged head.

"You OK for this?"

Ben nodded. He'd wrapped a single layer of gauze around his hands—enough to protect the palms while driving but not enough to interfere further with their flexibility.

Sly entered the conference room and wordlessly laid a short stack of copies in front of Ben. Ben knew they had to talk about the case, about John List. But he was at a loss at how to begin.

The conference room fell into sudden shadow, and he rose to open a blind and look out over the city. Clouds were stacked above the skyline and the treetops swayed—a sharp change from thirty minutes ago when the August sun beat through the car window like a hammer on an anvil, toasting his shoulder.

He sat and pulled the stack of printouts toward him.

"You don't want a meeting," he said. "I don't want a meeting. But we can't let this cool off."

The detectives straightened and Malone sat. Ben dismantled the stack of paper and slid the stapled sheets across the table.

"John List had his shooting spree in 1971. In the family mansion, a Victorian monstrosity called Breeze Knoll. His mother had revamped the attic floor into an apartment for herself. List was in his mid-forties, a mama's boy and religious nut. Said he believed his wife and three teen-aged children would go to hell if he didn't intervene. Left behind rambling notes that he was acting out of love and doing God's bidding. By killing his family now, they would die Christians and go to heaven."

Hilda's expression hardened. "If it was such a friggin' good idea, why didn't he off *himself?*"

"Good question. For religious freaks, it's always the mote in someone *else's* eye. What List's letters didn't discuss, however, was that he was a miserable failure who'd squandered the family fortune and accumulated a mountain of debt. He'd been selling the furniture out of the mansion— it was almost bare when the police found the bodies. And he'd accumulated a small arsenal.

"How to deal with the stress of personal failure— annihilate your family. And it *was* savage. List shot his 15-year-old son eight or nine times. Shoved his 86-year-old mother into an attic closet with such force that he snapped both her legs, then shot her pointblank in the face. To keep her from anguish, he said. He dragged the bodies of his wife and children into the ballroom and arranged them in the shape of a cross. And left them with organ music playing."

Proudhorse looked up from the printout. "Says here he was a control freak. And that he mowed the lawn in his suit and tie and dress shoes."

"What put you on to the List case, boss?" Hilda asked. "That quote?"

"Yes. Verbatim from List's note—*Mother is in the attic, she was too heavy to move.*" Ben paused. "Let's go to work. Again, we're looking for connections between the vics. Now we add the Oelanders."

"Except he didn't kill them," Proudhorse said as the team filed out.

Ben nodded but didn't say what he was thinking.
Maybe this one was for me.

He turned to the chief. "Funeral arrangements?"

"Looks like Friday. Everyone has out-of-state family. We want to memorialize all four officers at the same time."

Ben nodded, a bitter taste at the back of his throat. Better story for the media. As good a chief as Saenz was, he never stopped being political, never stopped thinking what would play best for the force.

They'd pull out all the stops. Ben imagined the cortege of motorcycle cops, the police helicopters whup-whupping overhead in V formation. The solid sea of dress blue punctuated with smartly saluting white gloves, black ribbons placed over badges—closing ranks behind the fallen heroes. The tolling church bell, riderless horses, twenty-one gun salute, the heart-rending playing of taps, the precisely folded American flags—mementos for the grieving . . . .

Not that their fallen four didn't deserve every bit of it—they did, singly and together. Ben thought of Charlaine, her soft *Hah, Bin.* All her bright promise, squandered. He was almost overwhelmed by a sudden wave of grief and guilt: Someone thought Ben led a "charmed life," so someone planned to destroy an entire family—randomly, a family of innocents. And someone *did* destroy four lives, equally innocent.

Ben's feelings crystallized into that cold, hard fact, into that resolve and purpose.

OK, he thought. Whatever it took.

CHAPTER THIRTY-FOUR

Tuesday afternoon, August 28

On the phone, Ted Oelander's voice was big and booming.

"So who has access to your schedule? Who knew you were going on vacation, for example?" Ben asked.

"Geez. Besides the whole world, you mean?"

"Just for purposes of elimination."

"Let's see. The people I work with knew. Relatives. Friends. Neighbors. People at church. The kids' teachers. Gardener. Mail guy. Paper guy."

"Somebody had to get past your security system. Did you call your security folks when you left?"

Oelander sounded sheepish. "We didn't turn the system on. Bonnie's sister is afraid of it and says she won't come into the house when that thing is on. So we didn't arm it. Thought she might need to get in the house to pick up something for the kids."

"Who else has a house key?"

"Dave Asquith, neighbor who kept our dog. And, uh— Bonnie's personal trainer."

Ben stopped doodling in his notebook.

"Does the trainer come to the house?"

"Sometimes. Usually, Bonnie goes to the center."

"Which center?"

"Zack's Fitness. It's on Pioneer—"

"I know where it is," Ben said. "What's the name of Bonnie's trainer?"

"Zack himself. He doesn't do much personal training since he bought the place. But Bonnie's been with him a long time."

"Mr. Oelander, I need to talk to you again asap, but in person. Tomorrow?"

"Geez, I have a full plate, insurance company and like that. And the police need to talk with us. Oh, that's right, you're the police."

"No, there will be routine police business—forms and the like. Someone will be in touch. But that's not what you and I will discuss. I'm Homicide."

The word *homicide* stopped Oelander, and when he spoke again, his buoyancy was gone.

"Will we be able to get into our house—or what's left of it?"

"No."

"Geez."

"Right now, it's a crime scene. I'm sorry."

"No, that's—"

"Can I reach you at this number?"

"My cell, yeah. And we'll stay with relatives. I can let you know."

"Mr. Oelander. You mentioned the people at your church a minute ago. What church do you attend?"

"A little Lutheran church up on—"

"That's OK," Ben said. "I'll be in touch. Let's try for Thursday."

#

It was midafternoon before Ben got to his weekend mail. Sly had placed yesterday's Cyberman note front and center on his desk. He read it without touching it. It was like the others. Mailed on Friday, black marker, block letters. Sly had slit the envelope's bottom and read the note to him only a little more than twenty-four hours ago, but it had the look and feel of old news.

OELANDER
DECEASED AUGUST 27
'MOTHER IS IN THE ATTIC.
SHE WAS TOO HEAVY TO MOVE.'

CHAPTER THIRTY-FIVE

Thursday, August 30

Chief Saenz stuck his head in Ben's office door.

"You say anything to Ken Akundi about what I told you?"

"Of course not."

"Well, don't."

"I wouldn't."

"I'm working on something," he said.

"Can I help?"

Ben's phone buzzed, and Ben picked it up, looking at the chief.

"No," Saenz said and went out the door.

"Lacefield stood us up," Pratt said on the phone.

Ben looked at his watch. "Where are you now?"

"Right out here. In the squad room."

Ben looked through the glass. Pratt sat at his desk, phone at his ear, gazing back at him.

"You've lost the use of your legs?"

"Well, the chief was with you, and I was . . . want me to come in there?"

"Why would you do that when we can talk on the phone and stare at one another through a window?"

"I'll come in there."

"Never mind, Pratt. I think I know where to find Lacefield."

#

"Swing through here," Ben said, sitting forward abruptly and indicating a driveway. "Here."

Kenechi spun the wheel hard to the right, and the unmarked lurched into the parking area for Eula's Home Cooking.

"Lonnie Lacefield lunches here," Ben explained. "Let's drive around the lot. Look for a big black SUV, plenty of chrome."

Kenechi cruised a little way into the lot and swept an all-inclusive hand toward the vehicles parked there. "Like these?"

"Good point. Let's go in."

Inside Eula's, Ben's eyes searched the lunch-hour crowd. He didn't see Lacefield. But he saw the fat guy in the smeared apron behind the counter.

"Remember me?" he asked, this time reaching for his badge.

"Naw, that's all right. Don't get out the badge. Gives the place a bad name." He glanced at Kenechi. "Brought reinforcements this time, eh?"

"He heard about your dinner rolls."

The counterman grinned and stuck out a hand. "I'm Eddie."

"The other day." Ben pointed in the direction of the big round table in the corner. "I asked you about a guy in Indian clothes. Sat over there."

"Lacefield?" Eddie ladled up some thick white gravy and thumped the ladle against the plate to dislodge it. "He was in here yesterday. Haven't seen him today."

Ben fished out a card and handed it to Eddie.

"You see him, tell him we're looking for him. Tell him if he's real smart, he'll call asap."

A pretty blonde in her twenties, cheeks flushed and rosebud mouth glossed in pink, hurried over with a pad and pencil.

"Just coffee," Ben said, adding to Kenechi under his breath, "Trust me."

"Me, too," Kenechi said.

The girl pocketed her pad, and Ben's glance fell on her ID badge.

"Trudelle," he said.

She looked back at him.

"Hold on a minute," he said. "Let me think."

He placed his fingertips on his forehead and rummaged around in his memory, the girl staring and Kenechi looking at him curiously.

She giggled. "So are you one of those claire . . . whatevers?"

Claire . . . Toby.

"Williams," Ben remembered. "Trudelle Williams."

Her grin fell away. "How could you know that?"

Ben pulled out his badge. "We're police, Trudelle. We need to talk to you."

Eddie came over to stand beside the girl, who looked scared.

"I didn't do anything," she said.

"What the hell," Eddie said.

"Is there someplace we can talk?" Ben asked.

"Hey, buddy," Eddie said. "It's lunch hour."

"Just a few questions," Ben said to the girl. "Nothing to worry about, Trudelle. It's about Toby Lugo."

Her eyes filled, a little *oh* on her glossy lips.

"Five minutes," Ben said to Eddie. "We wanted to talk to her anyway, and here she is."

216

Eddie looked around. Most of the diners were finishing, sitting back, full of grits and gravy and black-eyed peas.

"OK, fine, coupla minutes. You can take one of those booths." He gestured to a windowed wall in a small, cordoned-off adjoining room.

Trudelle moved ahead of them without speaking and scooted to the wall on one side of the booth. Ben slipped in opposite her, Kenechi beside. She huddled in the booth's corner, looking small and young and trapped.

"It's OK, Trudelle," Ben said, pulling out his notebook and laying it on the table in front of him.

She looked at the notebook, chin quivering.

"But I don't know anything."

"We got your name from Toby's parents. They just mentioned you as a friend."

"You're talking to his other friends?"

"You're the first. But we will."

She relaxed a little.

"Tell us about Toby."

"I can't believe what happened to him."

"I understand you were close in high school."

"Close to Toby? Well, yeah. But I knew him mostly through Lulie Boone."

"Lulie Boone? Who's that? A classmate?"

"Yeah. Sure. My best bud. They used to call us 'Tru and Lu.' Lulie Boone." She paused. "Lulu Ruben now."

Both detectives looked up from their notebooks.

"We always said she couldn't marry Toby Lugo when she graduated because her name would be Lulu Lugo." An uncertain smile pricked at her lips. "We thought it sounded like some African mumbo jumbo."

217

Misinterpreting their collective stare, she demonstrated—thrusting out her lips and saying roughly, "Lu lu lu go! Lu lu zu lu!" She let loose a burble of laughter, then broke off, eyes darting to the big black man at her side.

"Oh! I mean—" she said, pretty pink manicure flying to pretty pink lips. "I didn't mean—"

"Wait a minute," Ben said. "Trudelle. Toby Lugo was Lulu Ruben's boyfriend?"

"Huh? You kidding? Toby Lugo and Lulie Boone?" She pulled her gaze away from Kenechi and met Ben's eyes. "Big item. All through school—junior high, high school. We were all in the same grade. But when Lulie was a senior she fell for Zack Ruben. He was about the hottest guy in town. Older, too, out of school—made him all the hotter. They got married soon as Lulie graduated. She was preggers anyway."

Trudelle put her fingers to her lips again and averted her eyes. "With J.J."

A tear slid over her cheek. "I can't believe it," she whispered. "Lulie's old boyfriend got murdered, and so did her baby."

#

"I said, they went to school together," Ben said loudly into his mobile. He and Kenechi were outside Eula's, Ben talking to the chief. "Toby Lugo and J.J. Ruben's mother. They were childhood sweethearts."

Saenz took a minute to digest it. "So we've got that link. Finally. Any ties to Gaylord Daniel? Claire Craven?"

"We only just got this from Trudelle Williams, a classmate of Toby Lugo," said Ben, stepping out of the sun and into the shade of one of the live oaks lining the sidewalk. "We're still at Eula's, where Trudelle Williams works."

"What?"

"I said we're working on it."

"What's wrong with your phone?"

"I don't know. Something."

"Well, get it fixed. Or get a new one."

Ben eyeballed Kenechi and let his tongue loll from the corner of his mouth.

"You want me to fix my cell phone," he asked the chief, "or follow this lead?"

Saenz ignored his tone. "Get someone to go through the class rosters."

Ben clapped his phone shut.

"Sometimes," he said, shaking his head. "God almighty."

CHAPTER THIRTY-SIX

Thursday evening, August 30

Ben and Dayton were at Portofino, waiting for Nell, a half-finished bottle of Chilean red between them, the pianist tinkling away. Their table was next to a window overlooking Lincoln Square, the setting sun entering the window aslant and filtering through the lace curtain. The golden light mixed with the transient candlelight reminded Ben of a Vermeer painting. Or a Klimt. He glanced around the room and was immediately adrift on another memory—his last visit to Portofino. And Charlaine, approaching their table in a short white summer dress and wide white smile, saying *Hah, Bin* in her soft West Texas accent. With difficulty, he pulled himself back to the conversation.

"Sorry?"

"I said, do you think this connection between Toby Lugo and Lulu Ruben will help you solve the case?"

"It helps with what I've been puzzling over since this thing started. If these murders are the work of one person, how are the victims chosen or connected? And if they're *chosen*, that's not random. So if I can find their connections . . . In a nutshell, J.J. connects to Zack, Jiggy, Lulu—who, now we know, connects to Toby. So through Toby that whole contingent connects to the elder Lugos . . . ."

Ben continued his glum review until Dayton frowned.

"Sounds like six degrees of separation."

He removed his eyeglasses and gave them an unnecessary polish with his handkerchief.

"Ben, are you OK?"

"It's just—" Ben began, "I have this nagging feeling . . .
something I'm not seeing." He made an effort. "Still
planning to drive down to Huntsville Saturday and leave
Sunday?"

Dayton nodded.

"Early morning flight Sunday. If I'm delayed like last
time, at least I won't be getting in after midnight—"

Ben suddenly sat forward and gave Dayton a look of
such intensity that Dayton broke off and searched Ben's
face.

"What?"

Ben, staring into the middle distance, said *my god.*

"What."

"My god."

"Ben?"

Ben didn't move for a moment, then he made an
imaginary pistol with his index finger and thumb. Took
aim. Cocked his thumb and fired.

"Bingo," he said.

Pushing his wine glass aside, he tossed down his napkin
and rose.

"You've cracked it," Dayton said. He rose, too, signaling
the waiter that he'd be right back, and followed Ben
through Portofino's double doors. Outside, they stood
beneath a twilit sky black and noisy with birds looking for a
place to roost. Lincoln Square's trees, lined up like sentinels
along the walks and drives and patches of green, were
restless with their clamor. Calling raucously to each other,
the birds flitted from rooftop to treetop and aligned
themselves side by side on the power lines crisscrossing the
plaza.

"Looks like a scene out of a Hitchcock movie," Dayton said.

"They come every year, late summer, early fall," Ben said, feeling a surge of melancholy. "Summer's already over where they've been."

"What are you going to do?"

"I'm not sure."

"So it's less than proof."

Ben snorted. "Way less."

"But you know."

"I do."

"You feel it in your bones."

"I do." He shook his head. "The piece I missed. There all the time."

"Anything I can do?"

Ben shook his head.

"Are you—is there danger?"

Ben pulled out his car keys and met Dayton's eyes, worried behind the shining lenses. He laid a hand on the older man's shoulder, then stepped off the curb and strode toward the parking lot. He didn't know what he was going to do, but he was suddenly in a hurry to do it. Whatever it was, it might not be according to Hoyle—and he'd need backup. He pulled out his phone and punched Malone's speed-dial. After the fourth ring, he hung up, knowing the call was going to voice mail.

"Ben!" Dayton called after him, his tone urgent. "Be careful, son."

Dayton had called Ben "son" only rarely. And every time, it had touched Ben deeply. He glanced over his shoulder and raised a hand to Dayton, still in front of Portofino, looking after him in the gathering darkness, two fingers laid thoughtfully across his lips.

CHAPTER THIRTY-SEVEN

Ben slid behind the wheel and pulled out his notebook, leafed through it, found the number he wanted. A booming male voice answered.

"Mr. Oelander, this is Ben Gallagher. I have three questions that won't keep."

He backed out of his parking place while Ted Oelander talked, seeing in his rear view mirror Dayton still standing on the sidewalk in front of Portofino, looking after him. He queued up to exit Lincoln Square, barking questions at a puzzled Ted Oelander, who nevertheless answered without hesitation. Ben hung up, negotiated the turn onto Collins and jockeyed to get into the right lane, then tried Malone again. His phone dropped the call to Malone while it was still ringing. He tried Kenechi. No answer.

He groaned and tried again.

Like Ben, Kenechi kept himself available. So it was odd he didn't respond. But at least let Malone be there . . . .

He wasn't. Again, Ben bailed out on the fourth ring, trying twice more as he cruised down Collins, losing one call and the other going to his recording. OK. Kenechi again. Voice mail.

Christ!

Without a plan, Ben turned off Collins and headed west on Cain Place, coasted past 112, turned around, coasted past again. He turned again, this time pulling to the curb east of the house. The dusty blue pickup was in the drive. He wanted to see if—yes, there was a light on at the back of the bungalow. The front of the house was unlit, but Ben could see the roses massed darkly on the lattices separating the Craven place from its neighbor.

Engine running, he sat quietly, studying 112 Cain Place. But there was nothing to see—only the lights at the back of the house becoming more distinct as darkness fell. He sat long enough to call Kenechi and Malone again. He'd call the chief—he *should* call the chief—but say what? I have a hunch—no, better than a hunch—a lie, a bogus alibi. And Saenz would say: Great! As if this were just another development. He wouldn't realize Ben *knew*, wouldn't realize they had to act now before there was another victim. Why wouldn't he? Ben didn't know. But whenever he took the bit in his teeth, Saenz wouldn't let him run. Pulled him back as if they were headed for some precipice only *he* could see. *Wouldn't let him run!* And goddammit—when had Ben been wrong? He didn't invent the strumming at his middle, the pricking at his brain.

The light at the back of 112 went dark. Straining to see, Ben picked out a flash of white moving among the roses. Then nothing.

Pondering, his blood quick with an unnamed dread, he pulled away from the curb with his eye on 112. He cruised down Cain Place and rounded the corner onto Fielder. The phone in his lap rang.

It was Dayton.

"You get backup?"

"Not yet."

"Nell's freaking. Scared you'll go it alone."

Ben heard his mother's voice in the background.

"You called the chief?" Dayton asked.

"Let me get off the road, Dayt."

Ben's left palm throbbed from its grip on the steering wheel. He dropped the phone into his lap and, taking the wheel with both hands, steered the car into the next drive, a small, defunct shopping strip, and put the phone to his ear. Nobody was there. He punched the re-call button and there was Dayt, after a fragment of ring.

"My phone's not working right, Dayt. I'm—"

A dusty blue pickup raced by on Fielder, so fast Ben almost missed it. He dropped the phone again, spun the wheel hard, and pulled into Fielder's northbound traffic, narrowly missing a telephone pole on the right and an oncoming car on the left. The driver swerved into the far left lane and protested with intermittent blasts on the horn all the way to the next intersection. Ben tucked himself into the right-lane traffic and picked up the phone, knowing it would be dead.

It was.

Goddammit! He shouldn't have staked out the Craven place. Of course he would be seen! Especially for somebody who was watching. And he should've grabbed that missing piece of puzzle when it was handed to him more than a week ago. Stupid! Now, here he was, with no strategy, tailing the blue pickup. The long light at Randol Mill Road and Fielder went from yellow to red, the pickup sailing through at the last minute. Ben wavered for the millisecond it took to remember Charlaine and the others, and he floored it, speeding through on red. Now there could be no doubt for the pickup driver: The police were coming.

Ben set his chin. So be it. He felt for the phone's recall button, pressed it, waited, and shouted into his lap.

"Dayt!"

"I hear you."

"Call the chief. Ma has his numbers. If you don't get him, call the station. Tell them I need backup asap. Tell them it's the guy who killed our cops."

"Where are you going?"

The blue pickup sailed over the I-30 bridge, through the LaMar intersection, and headed for Temple Way Boulevard.

"I'm going to church."

#

The blue pickup was parked behind All Saints. Ben pulled in and sat for a second, his hands rigid on a steering wheel slick with serum from the blisters, willing his muscles to ease and heart to slow.

He scrutinized the L-shaped parking lot. The long stem of the L ran the full length of the west side of the building and the shorter base a little way behind the north side. Lights at both ends of the L's stem shone brightly on the building's west side, less so on the north and south, and left the east yard in darkness. That was the altar end of the building, Ben remembered, with stone steps leading to the heavy door that screeched on its brass jamb and three stained glass windows high on the wall.

Abraham and Isaac.

Ben took a small, shielded flashlight from the console and tested it against his palm. He had a larger version in the trunk, but the shielded beam would be better in this circumstance. He flicked off the car's dome light, opened the door quietly, and stepped out, his heels grating on the lot's loose gravel. Pushing the door gently until the latch caught, he moved around behind the blue pickup and peered into the empty bed. He bent to stare into the driver's window, leaning so close that his breath formed a small circle of mist on the glass.

Nothing to see.

He crept along the building's border of shrubs and rounded the northwest corner, where a narrow painted door was shrouded by a pair of cedars. The knob turned a little clockwise, then caught and held. Locked. He turned and inspected this side of the building. Its long stained glass windows were lit dimly from within, but from where he stood at ground level, they were above his head. Even if they were lower, he wouldn't be able to see through the heavily colored glass.

He kept moving, across the walk leading to the front entrance and up the steps, listening. Small amber lights mounted on either side of the wide entry provided little light, but the building's front was softly illuminated by light from the parking lot. Ben shone the flashlight on the brass door handles. The double doors were secured by a deadbolt. He grasped the handle and pressed the thumbturn gently. It moved downward, then stopped. Also locked.

He heard a sudden restless murmur, a rustling, and remembering the flight of bats on that Tuesday night walk with Bood, he backed down the steps and craned his neck to see the triangular ventilator slats beneath the eaves. Scores of tiny dark forms flitted erratically from beneath the eaves, speeding unerringly to the dictates of their sonar.

He sprinted back to the grass strip close to the building and slipped around the corner. The only entry on the building's east side was the heavy planked door at the northeast corner. But Ben knew that even if it were unlocked, its scrape would announce his entrance.

The altar side of the church lay in deep shadow and he strained to listen, to see. The graveyard caught some light from the parking lot—he could make out pale rectangles of tombstones on the other side of the iron fence, banked by Duff Craven's red roses. But the wall and its immediate yard were dark, and Ben's flashlight would do little to illumine the wall's length. He squinted into the churchyard, where the oblique beam of the parking lot lights lengthened the restless shadows and laid them on the lawn as if on the wall of Plato's cave.

There was a swishing sound behind him, and he swung around, scalp prickling. A bicycle sped past the front of All Saints, the rider in reflective racing gear and bent low over the handlebars, breathing hard, wheels flashing by with only that slight whir.

Ben exhaled and tried to slow the clamor in his chest. He was damp with sweat, every sense alert, mouth dry, hair on his forearms raised a little.

A car crested Fielder hill, its lights pointing toward him briefly then swinging east, down Temple Way Boulevard. But in that instant, Ben turned and scrutinized the briefly lit side yard and east wall.

Then the car was gone, Ben's vision taking a moment to adjust, red imprints of the headlights on the insides of his eyelids—but also the image of the church wall and the stair leading to the door. Nothing. He sprinted across the lawn, mounted the stone steps, seized the thumbturn of the latch, and pressed.

The thumbturn moved all the way. Unlocked!

Now. The only way to avoid that shriek of wood against metal was to lift the heavy oaken door enough to clear the jamb. Ben took off his suitcoat and draped it over the iron rail—freeing his arms and shoulders and also giving him access to the Glock strapped to his chest.

He stiffened his back and braced his knees. Grabbing the handle with both hands, ignoring the pains shooting across his blistered palms, he lifted straight up, putting his all into it, grunting, feeling the door move upward and inward slightly, silently. He paused, still holding the door, and prepared himself for another fraction of an inch, braced, grabbed his breath, and pulled.

The door budged inward slightly and at that instant—holding its weight in his damaged palms—Ben felt something press against his leg. Startled, he lurched to the left and looked down. The rough-looking tortoiseshell cat, the All Saints cat with the brindled orange and black fur, was leaning against his leg. Ben felt a millisecond of relief—then, as he held the door, a pain unlike any he had ever known ripped the length of his back. He buckled, almost screamed.

The door fell its fraction of an inch and rasped loudly over the jamb, swinging ajar, the cat winding past Ben's legs and dashing into the dim interior on silent feet.

Ben froze, hearing nothing but his own ragged breath, nothing but eerie quiet from the sanctuary. After a tiny space of listening, of waiting for the pain to ebb, he pulled his gun from its holster—tried to hold it in his right hand securely, naturally, disregarding pain. But the weapon felt like a foreign object against his swollen, stiffened palm.

He took a breath, exhaled, and stepped inside.

CHAPTER THIRTY-EIGHT

A soft light came from the sanctuary, but no sound, no sense of presence. He took a step from the wall, testing his back. Every move hurt.

At the tall archway leading to the sanctuary, he peered into the dim chamber.

Ricky Craven stood behind the altar, beneath the trio of stained glass windows. He was looking at Ben. Waiting.

"Taking care of the sacred objects, Ricky?"

Ricky's face was impassive but his eyes burned with a peculiar excitement—a flame Ben had seen before. He tried to arrange his own expression so it wasn't a transparent mask of pain.

Ricky stepped from behind the altar, his braced leg clumsy on the red carpet.

"Working late?"

"I had a revelation." Ben's voice sounded unnatural even in his own ears.

Ricky paused and tilted his head.

"You're smart, Ricky, but not smart enough."

"You mean I'm smart but not lucky, don't you, detective? But everybody knows I'm not lucky. That's no revelation. Luck. *Your* province."

Feeling as mechanical as a stick figure, Ben moved gingerly down the three steps to the nave. He skirted the stair leading to the apse and maneuvered around the front section of pews and down the nave's center aisle, holding his gun at his side.

"Is this where you assisted Gaylord Daniel, Ricky?"

Ricky turned, Ben noting again his resemblance to his mother—the smoldering, deep-set dark eyes, almost almond-shaped above the high cheekbones, the mobile, feminine mouth and its lush lower lip.

"Gaylord," Ricky said agreeably. "What a great name that man had. Gay Lord. Perfect."

"Except he wasn't gay, was he."

"He was whatever was expedient."

"He preferred your mother to you."

"He preferred anyone to me. You think *that* was a problem? I hated him—hated him as much as I hated my mother. And he hated me right back. I was so much less than perfect."

He touched the thin white scar that angled from his upper lip to his nostril.

"Especially this. Said it reminded him of a cloven hoof."

The Glock felt slippery in Ben's grasp—the blisters leaking serum.

"For that, you killed him."

"He died to accompany my mother. They were a couple. The supreme cause."

"The others providing cover. One of your mistakes."

"*One* of my mistakes. Name another."

A wave of pain and nausea washed over Ben, and he realized he was clinging hard to his Glock on the right and to the oaken back of a pew on the left.

Ricky was gazing at him expectantly. Ben fought his way through a red-black fog.

"Name another."

"Your alibi. You said you heard the planes queuing up for a southerly approach that Sunday—when the wind shifted."

Ricky almost smiled. "At midnight."

"If you heard the planes change their approach, you were not at home as you said—and out of hearing range— but right here, until well after the murders."

"Good catch. Name another."

"Fuck you, Craven," Ben had to struggle to keep from panting. "This isn't a game."

Ben set his foot on the raised platform of the chancel, mounted the step, and with that small motion, his wounded back walloped him again, felling him like an oak. He dropped to all fours on the carpeted aisle, his weight falling on his burned palms and the gun slipping from his grasp.

Ben's range of vision was limited in this position, but he could see Ricky's advance, his built-up shoe with the brace fitted onto its instep. Ben grabbed vainly at the choir rail, and failing to push back onto his knees, strained to pull up his head and look at Ricky—who returned his gaze quizzically, a slender finger over his red lips.

"What a time for that pesky back to act up, eh, Gallagher?" He stepped closer, kicked the Glock out of reach, and prodded Ben's torso with the toe of his shoe.

"Oh dear," he said. "The hunter as crippled as his prey."

Ben tried to shift his weight to his trembling arms. But Ricky gave him a hard shove with his foot, and he fell over onto his side, knees still bent, his right arm clamped beneath him. He tried to raise his torso and was rewarded with a jolt of pain. But it was no longer only pain. Ben tried to shift his legs and realized he couldn't. He tried again. The lower half of his body was immobile.

Ben could hear the slurry sound of Ricky's brace moving over the carpet, could hear his rapid, shallow breathing. Ricky moved into view, and Ben saw the ax. Ricky pointed the ax toward one of the stained glass windows above the altar—the bound Isaac, the angel staying Abraham's knife.

"Where's *your* angel, detective? And aren't you a tasty dish to set before the King."

He brought the ax blade to Ben's face; Ben felt it as a heavy cold line diagonally across his cheek.

"Blood of the lamb." Ricky's voice was tremulous. He turned the ax in both hands, his face wearing an expression Ben didn't recognize. Whatever it was—ecstasy, excitement—it made Ben consolidate all his strength into one place, center it in his arms and gut and shoulders. He seized the legs of the pew nearest his head and prepared to roll and pull himself beneath the pew.

Ricky came fast, the brace dragging on his leg, but not slowing him much. Ben, lying aslant in the aisle, saw Ricky arch directly overhead, saw the ax moving up and descending. And with all his might, he rolled over, feeling the glancing blow of the ax, its blade slicing into the flesh and muscle of his upper arm.

Ben pulled at his maimed arm and rolled again beneath the oaken pew, which took a hard, thudding blow from Ricky's ax. Ben kept moving, sliding against the polished wood beneath the pews, the next pew and the next withstanding the blows from the ax—pulling himself with one burned hand, his injured arm pumping blood, moving by inches when he needed yards. Ricky appeared between the pews, clumsily dragging his braced leg into the narrow space, lifting the ax.

"Ricky! No!" The cry rang out at the top of the ax's arc. Duff Craven appeared in the aisle, holding Ben's Glock straight out, only feet from his son.

Then Ricky, his voice soft as a child's.

"You going to shoot me, Dad?"

Duff's face was ravaged. "She was your mother."

"She was—"

"She was your mother! I loved her. As much as I love you."

"Dad." Ricky lowered the ax and put out a hand—Ben silently scooting, grabbing a pew, pulling himself beneath it like an auto mechanic beneath a car.

Abruptly, Ricky jerked the ax up with both hands, and Ben saw the blade at the top of its swing and knew whatever he had left wasn't going to be enough. Then an explosion and a bright burst of red blew away from the right side of Ricky's head, his jelly doughnut mouth forming a bright O as he fell obliquely between the pews and onto Ben like an ardent lover.

Duff stepped into the narrowing margin of Ben's vision and tugged at his son, wrestled him into his arms as he might a bag of seed, and staggered from view. Ben was adrift on an ocean of shock and pain when Duff reappeared, bending near, his face a blurred oval framed by stained glass—by Abraham's sacrifice.

Ben, his torso bright with blood, tried to sit up.

"Lie still," Duff said. "Help is on the way."

He fell to his knees beside Ben.

"My hands." He sobbed. "I almost couldn't pull the trigger."

Hands as maimed as mine, Ben thought. And the world fell away.

CHAPTER THIRTY-NINE

Friday, August 31

"That's all I remember," Ben told Nell, who stood at his hospital bedside.

"An ax, Ben. Jesus Christ, an *ax*. Why can't you—" She sent an appealing glance across the room, where Kenechi Akundi sat, a newspaper on his crossed knees and face shining blue-black in the window's morning light.

Someday Ben would ask him about that scar.

"He has a doctorate, Kenechi. Why can't he be a professor or something."

Both men grinned.

"What," Nell said.

"Ken has a doctorate, too, Ma. Chemical engineering."

"Honest to god. You cops." She shook her head. "In a week, Ben, you sliced your knuckles putting your fist through a window. Got a concussion from being hit on the head. Burned your hands in a bomb blast. Were attacked with an ax. *And* had back surgery. I hope you learned something from this last week."

Ben regarded her calmly.

"I did. I learned that control goes to those who can. And even those who *can* can't control everything."

It wasn't the response she expected.

"What are we talking about?"

"Wait a minute," Ben said. "I had *back* surgery?"

"L five, Benny. The last lumbar vertebra. Which you damaged when you fell down the Blums' staircase all those years ago. What happened last night was a piece broke off

236

that disk and embedded itself in the nerve. That's why you couldn't move."

"The paralysis was scarier than the pain." Ben shifted himself, marveling. He almost couldn't remember a time when his back didn't hurt.

"Microsurgery," Nell said. "Took less than half an hour. Surgeon said all he did was remove that fragment. Incision's only about an inch long."

She laid her hand lightly on the bundle of bandage over his shoulder.

"This took a hell of a lot longer." She sighed. "One of these days I'm going to ask why you went to that church by yourself. But don't get me started."

"Count on me, Ma."

Kenechi said, "We were on the way, but Duff Craven called nine-one-one, and they got to you first."

"Duff's OK?" Ben asked.

Nell frowned.

"OK? Of course he's not OK. His son killed his mother. He killed his son. Duff Craven has lost everything. He will never be OK. And it's a damned shame. He's a decent man. As crippled in his way as his son, but—"

She studied Ben, eyes filling. "How could Ricky Craven do such things, Ben?"

"He blamed his mother—"

He turned to Kenechi.

"That phone conversation Regina Tupp told us about? It was Ricky, not Duff, who was stalking Claire. It was Ricky she was afraid of. Claire's remark that she was turning to stone, her reference to the tears of Niobe . . . that myth had a different meaning for her. She cried not because her child died, but because he lived—and lived maimed, a daily accusation. Claire wanted an abortion and when Duff stood in her way, she tried to get rid of Ricky. His birth defects may or may not have been her fault. But she thought they were. And so did Ricky. From what Regina and Lily said, I'd guess Verlie Mae Cheek said as much to Ricky. She was malicious enough to say it, and he was bitter enough to believe it."

A wave of tiredness washed over Ben, and he paused.

Kenechi said, "Claire was Ricky's target, and the serialist thing was just a cover."

"If his other victims really had been random, it might have worked. But he decided, as long as he was looking for sensational murder cases, to look for cases that would help him settle an old score—revenge for a high school romance gone sour. Ricky loved Lulu Ruben in his twisted way. So he wanted to hurt not only her, but the two men she preferred—Toby Lugo and Zack Ruben."

"So it wasn't Ricky who was providing an alibi for Duff, but the other way around."

"Not because Duff thought Ricky was guilty of murder, though." Ben said. "Not at first. Duff showed up at All Saints last night because he'd begun to wonder. I saw something in his face I couldn't read when I showed him the purple ribbon that had bound Claire's love letters. Now I know it was suspicion. Duff probably thought Claire had taken the letters with her that Sunday night. But she wouldn't have untied the bundle and left the ribbon in the drawer. Someone untied them to read them, then took them away, forgetting the ribbon. Duff knew he was not that person. And that left Ricky."

Ben drifted a little, and he wondered what was dripping into his veins.

"How did you know, Ben?" Nell asked.

"Dayt mentioned his flight getting in late the night Gaylord Daniel and Claire—" He broke off. "Where is Dayton, anyway?"

"He's at your house with Bood. Left while you were in Recovery."

"Is he OK?"

"Dayton or Bood?"

"Both of them," he said, shamefaced that he'd meant Bood.

Nell nodded, smiling at him with her eyes.

"Dayt reminded me that the front came through around midnight the Sunday Claire and Daniel were killed," Ben said. "And later Ricky said he'd heard the planes queuing up for a southerly approach when the wind shifted. But if he heard that, he was at All Saints at midnight, well past the time he said he'd gone home. And past the time his mother and Gaylord Daniel were shot in the churchyard — shots unheard in the clamor of fireworks from the ballpark."

Ricky setting out the trash that Tuesday night, Ben remembered. He'd have put his bloody clothing in those bags. And maybe Claire's wedding rings. And her tongue. Like a bad piece of meat. Spraying the bags with ammonia. Couldn't have critters running down the street with his mother's tongue.

"Ricky delivered *The New York Times*. When I left Portofino last night, I called Oelander and asked three questions. Do you subscribe to *The New York Times*? Did you stop it during your vacation? Do you happen to know your deliverer's name?"

"Yes on all counts," Kenechi said.

"Right. When the Oelanders stopped the paper, they told Ricky they'd be gone, when, and for how long. It gave him access. He booby-trapped the Oelander place and set us up. Incidentally, Ricky Craven also delivered my *New York Times*. And he broke into my place the day of the Oelander explosion. Left me flowers and a personal note of admiration."

"My god, Ben! I wish—" Nell was interrupted by a mocha-skinned nurse who wore a closely cropped cap of frizz and bustled into the room carrying a little tray.

Ben grinned. "Ratched! That you?"

"Sure enough is," she said, busying herself with pulse and temperature. "You doin' OK?"

She gently tugged the dressing from his tonsured head and peered at the staples, murmuring.

"Could you look at his burns?" asked Nell. "And he has stitches on his knuckles."

"I brought something for that." Ratched sprayed Ben's blisters with something from an aerosol container, patted them dry, smeared on ointment, and laid on some gauze.

"Take off the gauze when that ointment's absorbed." She pulled out the drawer on the bedstand. "All your stuff in here?"

"Looks like it."

Ratched smoothed his sheets and drew closer.

"You drew my picture real good."

She stepped to the closet and pulled out the large plastic bag that held Ben's blood-soaked clothing. Tucked the bag under her arm and turned to Nell.

"This time," she indicated the plastic bag, "this time if your boy sneak out the hospital, he gonna be naked."

Nell watched her leave the room. "I won't pretend to know what that was about. I'm going to go, Benny. You sleep. I just want to say thank God for Duff Craven."

"Saved my life," Ben said. "And with my gun, too."

"Good job someone knew how to use it."

"I thought you weren't going to start, Ma. But since you have—we stopped a killer, Ma. Don't you think that's a real job, as you put it? We solved four murders. Make that eight murders—with Charlaine and Coy and Pearl and Hanna. No, make it ten. Because we're also gonna get the guy who killed the Blum brothers. Wait. Make it eleven. Because that'll be LeRoy Shatto's killer, too. *Eleven, Ma.*"

She looked at Kenechi for corroboration.

He gave her a white smile.

"So how was *your* week, Ma?" Ben asked.

#

Ben woke to a rustling across the room. Kenechi folding his newspaper.

"You still here?" Ben said.

"I wanted to give you this. From the chief."

Ben reached into the gift bag and withdrew a new cell phone.

"They got it all set up. Chief says you can tinker with it while you're lying here."

Ben examined the phone. "Probably bugged."

Kenechi grinned.

"I won't be lying here long, Kenechi. I gotta be out for Andrew's parole, gotta be ready."

"Is it going to happen?"

"Yes."

"You're sure of that."

"Yes."

Kenechi paused. "You feel it in your bones?"

"I do."

And he did. *Andrew's coming home.* He felt the weight of a decade lifting from his shoulders. His baby brother—the big laugh and easy spirit, the hazel eyes with their brush of reddish lash, the freckled skin—all of it rushed through him like a stream from a broken dam. Free. Andrew Gallagher—as Jack Malone had called him in better days, the star of our lives.

Ben remembered something.

"Did Malone ever call you last night?"

"He left a message. Finally. Sounded wasted. When I called back, there was no answer. Not at home or on his mobile."

"I know what that's like."

"Ben. Grace and I were out celebrating, and I shut off my mobile. I know that's not good policy, but I risked it for a couple of hours. A couple of critical hours, as it turned out. It was a bad decision. I'm sorry."

Ben waved it away.

"I've made a few bad decisions, Ken. And it's only Rolando Saenz who expects you to be on call twenty-four-seven. You were celebrating?"

"Grace is pregnant."

Ben didn't try to act surprised. "So there'll be another little Akundi running around. Congratulations."

"I wasn't sure I could swing it. But I got a fellowship at Texas Christian University—"

"Shit," Ben said.

"—teaching a Saturday seminar for a few semesters. Chief okayed it. Has a nice stipend that'll tide us over. Also—"

"You're not quitting?"

"*Also*," Kenechi said, brushing aside Ben's question. "The chief said I should tell you—"

Ben waited.

"I'm being promoted. Detective sergeant. Means a nice raise."

"Is he going to give you my job, too? Or just my rank?"

"Probably just getting me in line for the next time you screw up a case."

Ben couldn't move his bandaged arm, so he stuck out his left hand—thinking as he grasped Kenechi's huge, leathery paw that it was like shaking with a catcher's mitt.

"The chief didn't bitch and moan and cry *ay yi yi* about my going it alone last night?"

"Well, yeah, that. But he said to go ahead and—"

Ben broke in. "Take a few days off?"

"How'd you know?"

"Tomorrow's Saturday," Ben said.

"And the next day's Sunday."

"And the next day's Labor Day."

You could hear Kenechi's soprano laughter all the way down the hall. Ben loved the sound of it.

* * *

FROM *MONKEY SEE* TO *CHALK LINE* . . .

Monkey See is a prequel to *Chalk Line*, which introduced Paula LaRocque's unforgettable detective, Ben Gallagher.

In *Chalk Line*, Gallagher is on a case that will change his life. He thinks his family will be restored when his brother, Andrew, gets out of Huntsville Prison. But on that long-awaited day, the brothers discover the body of a dear friend, a murder that launches Ben on a fast slide from his revered rule of law. It's bad enough that his superiors warn him off the case—but, worse, the closer he gets, the surer he is that his family is implicated. Torn between loyalties, he embarks on a race to catch a killer that takes him thousands of miles and a couple of decades away—to a cold case in the north that leads to a killer no one would ever think to suspect.

Excerpts from reviews of *Chalk Line:*

"*Chalk Line* is a smart, snappy, knot-tight novel that keeps you on the edge of your seat and of Paula LaRocque's limber imagination. Nietzsche-quoting detectives, Texas-sized oddballs, delicious family secrets, the hot trail of a killer (and an icy cold one from crimes long ago) – all of these are spun into a chilling (and comical) yarn of murder and mayhem. *Chalk Line* is guaranteed to startle, to entertain, and to challenge your beliefs about the true nature of justice."
—Stuart Wilk, producer of the musical "Yank!" and former managing editor of *The Dallas Morning News*

"Absorbing . . . delivers a complicated, satisfying mystery tale. . . . Deftly avoids the easy, larger-than-life 'Texas' stereotypes that infect many detective novels set in the Lone Star State. . . . An engrossing, entertaining detective tale and a good down payment on future Ben Gallagher mysteries."—*The Dallas Morning News*

"LaRocque has created a handful of appealing characters with detailed backstories to begin her series, and it's well worth getting in at the start."—*Booklist*

"*Chalk Line* is a fast, smart read, a meaty morality tale with complicated characters and shades of gray." —*Denton Record-Chronicle*

"A completely different kind of mystery." —*Fort Worth Star-Telegram*

"Ben Gallagher is a great new character. The plot is seamless and suspenseful. And best of all, the writing is superb. No surprise there because the author of "Chalk Line" is one of the greatest writing coaches of all time. Now that I've finished the first Ben Gallagher mystery, I can't wait for the next one."
—Bruce DeSilva, Edgar Award-winning author of *Rogue Island*

"Obviously well-written (LaRocque practices what she preaches)." —*Abilene Reporter-News*

"*Chalk Line* is at once a spellbinding mystery and a serious work of fiction—one that plumbs the meaning of family and explores the wavering line between justice and the law. A stunning debut from a writer who is going places." (jacket blurb)
—Bruce DeSilva, Edgar Award-winning author of *Rogue Island*

"Make way for a big new talent in mystery fiction. Paula LaRocque writes like a dream, and her story's twists and

turns will keep you up at night, turning pages. When Ben Gallagher is on the case, readers are in for a great treat."
—Doug J. Swanson, author of the Jack Flippo mystery series and of the recently released biography of Texas-born casino owner and mobster Benny Binion

"Cops, murderers, and Texas – a great mix from which Paula LaRocque creates an imaginative, gripping story that is sure to delight mystery devotees."
—Philip Seib, Professor of Journalism and Director of the Center on Public Diplomacy, University of Southern California

Excerpts from Amazon.com Reader Reviews:

"This was an absolutely great read — could not put it down! A true page-turner and the first of what I hope to be a long series of Gallagher mysteries."

LaRocque's "vibrant descriptions of North Texas places and people are worth the price of admission. But, even better, she spins a great yarn. And, when the action shifts to the Midwest, the story takes on an intensity and emotional depth worthy of the most discriminating reader. I heartily recommend this book. If there is a mystery lover in your life, this is your Christmas purchase."

"I'm anxiously awaiting the next book in the series."

"Very well written and interesting characters with a great ending."
"The author knows how to grasp the meaning of family vs. job and family vs. law."

"I'm . . . telling all my friends to read *Chalk Line*."

Praise for

THE BOOK ON WRITING: THE ULTIMATE GUIDE TO WRITING WELL

by Paula LaRocque

For more than a decade, Paula LaROCQUE's *Book on Writing* has helped thousands become clear and polished writers overnight. When LaRocque—considered by many one of the world's great writing coaches—published the book in 2003, she had just wrapped up a 20-year stint as writing coach at *The Dallas Morning News*. At publication, the book was chosen by the American Booksellers Association for its Top Ten list as well as for the highly influential "Book Sense 76" list. The Writer's Web Watch also named it No. 1 of the top six books published that year. Here's a short sample of excerpts from early reviews:

"LaROCQUE's advice is sane and sound. . . . Beginning writers should find clear, useful advice here."
—*Publishers Weekly*

"A clear and concise guide." *(Kindle Edition)*
—*Library Journal*

"Paula LaRocque offers her impressive expertise in *The Book On Writing: The Ultimate Guide To Writing Well* . . . an excellent and highly recommended guide to clarity of thought and printed word."
— *Midwest Book Review*

"Paula LaRocque understands that the way to elegant, artful storytelling is simple, basic, accurate words used sparingly and with purpose. She demonstrates why clarity, simplicity, and dignity top flabby construction and corpulent descriptives every time. *The Book on Writing* is THE book on writing."
—Bob Giles, curator, Nieman Foundation for Journalism, Harvard University

"This book is well-organized, cleanly written, and keenly insightful. It embraces the whole of writing—whether of great novelists or office managers . . . This is really good and useful stuff."
— Allen Pusey, editor and publisher
ABA Journal, American Bar Association

"Don't waste your time arguing with Paula LaRocque's advice. Just read, learn, and do. It's a guarantee you WILL write well and your readers will get well in the process."
—Tom Sylvestri, president
Community Newspapers, Media General, Inc.

About the Author

Paula LaRocque was assistant managing editor and writing coach at *The Dallas Morning News* for 20 years. She also taught writing at Western Michigan, Texas A&M, Southern Methodist, and Texas Christian universities. She worked as a consultant for the Associated Press; the Drehscheibe Institute in Bonn, Germany; the European Stars & Stripes, and for many other institutions, businesses, publications, and government agencies. In 2001, she received the Associated Press Managing Editors Association's Meritorious Service Award for Exemplary Contribution to Journalism. Her columns on writing have appeared regularly in *Quill* magazine for nearly 25 years. She has authored three nonfiction books—including her popular 2003 work, *The Book on Writing: The Ultimate Guide to Writing Well.* Reviewers praised her first fiction, *Chalk Line,* a Ben Gallagher mystery published in 2011.

Learn more on the official site

You can also find her on Facebook and Twitter.

www.ingramcontent.com/pod-product-compliance
Lightning Source LLC
Chambersburg PA
CBHW020756250626
47155CB00003B/1096